Midnight Cartel 3

Chris Green

Lock Down Publications and
Ca$h
Presents
Midnight Cartel 3
A Novel by *Chris Green*

Chris Green

Lock Down Publications
P.O. Box 944
Stockbridge, Ga 30281

Visit our website @
www.lockdownpublications.com

Lock Down Publications
Like our page on Facebook: Lock Down
Publications @
www.facebook.com/lockdownpublications.ldp
Cover design and layout by: **Dynasty Cover Me**
Book interior design by: **Shawn Walker**
Edited by: **Jill Alicea**

Stay Connected with Us!

Text **LOCKDOWN** to 22828 to stay up-to-date with
new releases, sneak peaks, contests and more…
Thank you.

Submission Guideline.

Submit the first three chapters of your completed manuscript to ldpsubmissions@gmail.com, subject line: Your book's title. The manuscript must be in a .doc file and sent as an attachment. Document should be in Times New Roman, double spaced and in size 12 font. Also, provide your synopsis and full contact information. If sending multiple submissions, they must each be in a separate email.

Have a story but no way to send it electronically? You can still submit to LDP/Ca$h Presents. Send in the first three chapters, written or typed, of your completed manuscript to:

LDP: Submissions Dept
Po Box 944
Stockbridge, Ga 30281

DO NOT send original manuscript. Must be a duplicate.

Provide your synopsis and a cover letter containing your full contact information.

Thanks for considering LDP and Ca$h Presents.

Acknowledgements and Dedication

This book right here is for the princess of the family, Cerenity Green. The Queen Dolsellia Green. My bruddas DeAngelo Green, Timothy Johnson, Jerome Martin, Robert Bell, Siddiq. All y'all mean the world to me. Wild child and Mayhem. Y'all too, li'l bro. I've been pushing to get home, and now this chance has finally presented itself. The OsaGang Movements is in full effect, and I'm glad to have all of y'all present while I'm doing this. Book #15, and there are plenty more to go. Shout out to the entire Green family: my uncle Kevin, my auntie Candies, Melita Michelle, Shanika, Yanna my grandmother and my great-grandmother Dianna, and Doris. I love you Queens so much. I just want everybody to know that. We're on lockdown right now and have been for twenty-one days. It's hard, but through Allah, everything is possible and will get better. The talented Alexus Breanna, thank you, ma!

This book is dedicated to my OsaGang brother Sip. I hate that you never got a chance to make it back to the streets. You died on this lockdown from the hands of another brother, so I know you are guaranteed Paradise. Your blood will not be lost in vain. We love you forever, li'l bro. Insh'allah, you will be amongst the other martyrs.

Chris Green

Chapter 1
Demerea's spot, 7:43 a.m.

Ryan cracked his eyes from the sound of his phone buzzing repeatedly. His vision was cloudy from the night before, and his body felt stiff as a bowl of cold grits. He rolled his eyes over to Demerea, who laid next to him with her back heaving lightly. Ryan moved her arm and sat up. Her nude body quickly caught his attention, forcing him to check himself. His boxers and pants were sprawled out on the floor, and the sound of his cell buzzing on the nightstand started to bubble up a strong-ass headache.

Ryan snatched up his boxer briefs and pants, put his clothes back on, and picked up the Samsung touchscreen. Thirteen missed calls were floating at the top of his screen, including six missed calls from his associate. When Precious crossed the edge of his mind, Ryan silently cursed to himself. Standing up, his head began to instantly thump in pain. Using an index finger to massage his temple, he looked back at Demerea and shook her leg lightly.

"Ay, wake up."

Stirring from her sleep, Demerea pulled the blanket smoothly over her soft skin. "What it do, big man?" Demerea smirked seductively.

"What the fuck happened last night?"

"What do you mean? You said that we could talk in the room, and that's exactly what we did. I rode that dick in a circle." She cheesed harder than a kid with a handful of dollar bills.

"My shit is thumping. I was supposed to be back at my crib in Philly. Ain't no way I fell asleep and didn't know what the fuck I was doing because I ain't drank nothing but three cups of liquor. Did you put something in my shit?" Ryan gave her a cold scowl.

"Nigga, stop fucking playing with me. Yo' lovey dovey ass wanted some pussy and ended up falling asleep afterwards. Don't blame me because you can't handle a couple of drinks, boy!" Demerea snapped.

The sound of his phone buzzing again caused him to answer it quickly. "Yeah, wassup, man?"

"Ryan, where are you, bro? Do you know what's going on right now?" Nas questioned. His tone was low as if he was trying to keep a secret.

"I'm at DJ's spot. I crashed here last night. Why?"

"Because I been out in front of your spot in Philly since this morning, and the police are surrounding yo' crib. It's a dead girl in front of your door, homie," he alerted Ryan.

"What?"

"Yeah, the folks are in yo' shit right now. They have a Lexus sectioned off with crime scene evidence tape and all kinds of stuff."

Hearing "Lexus" made his mind shift towards Precious. The nasty bubble gut feeling began again in his stomach. "Nas? What color is the car?" Ryan asked calmly, trying not to panic.

"It's a white one, homie."

The cringe that rushed over his flesh caused his heart to sink. "I'm on the way!" he shouted before hanging up the line.

"What's wrong?" Demerea looked at him nervously.

"I think something is wrong with Precious," he mumbled while shuffling to put his shoes on.

It didn't take Demerea long to jump out of the bed to follow his lead. Grabbing a pair of sweatpants and slides, she moved out of the bedroom behind him.

Ryan woke DJ up from the living room couch. Ryan gave him a second to snatch up his things, and then they left Demerea's crib. The small ride over the Delaware Bridge didn't take long, and Ryan was pumping the gas down the road perfectly in order to reach his destination. It didn't take longer than twenty-five minutes before Ryan reached the bottom of his street. When he turned inside the narrow section, he saw the authorities crawling around every section of the area. The early birds were still chirping, and these people were moving about dusting every section of the street they could. The police taking a photo of Precious's car caught Ryan's eye, forcing him to pull over in the middle of his block and approach the first officer he saw.

"Excuse me, this is my apartment. What's going on?"

DJ and Demerea couldn't help but to climb out behind him.

The young black rookie officer looked him up and down before replying. "You're the owner of this home?"

"I just said that, didn't I? What the fuck is going on? Why are these people in my crib?" Ryan looked around to see what all his pupils could spot out.

"Well, a woman was shot in front of your home last night, sir. We were wondering if you may know her. Her ID reads as Precious Edmond."

The sound of her sweet angelic name was the last thing he heard before slightly spazzing out. Ryan reached out for the officer's neck in anger, forcing DJ to grab him. "Tell me you lying, motherfucker. She not dead. Tell me you lying." Ryan pointed at him sternly. The tears had already begun to slide down his face.

It was obvious the rookie enforcement officer didn't want to escalate the situation. He waved for his supervisor. He whispered a few words into his ear and allowed him to take over.

"Hi, my name is Detective Ross. Which one of you would be the owner of this home?" He looked between all three of them.

"Me," Ryan mustered with his head down in defeat.

The detective cleared his throat before speaking again. "I can see that this woman was obviously someone special to you. Maybe you can help us, because we're wondering who would pull a stunt like this, upon a college student, at that. We've been investigating since last night and still haven't come up with an explanation," he informed them.

"Oh my God! Faith," Demerea said with a hand covering her mouth.

Ryan jerked his head back after her remark slipped out. "What do you mean 'oh my God, Faith'? Did that bitch have something to do with this?" Moving closer to her, Ryan grabbed her arms. "Demerea, I asked you a question!"

"I don't know, Ryan! I don't know!" she shouted with tears welling at the corners of her eyelids. "Last night, Faith was really angry. It's like all she could speak on was hurting Precious. I've never seen her talk that way, but I didn't think she was serious," Demerea stuttered in fear.

"Um, who is Faith?" Detective Ross tuned his ears into their conversation.

Ryan was careful not to say the wrong thing, knowing that the streets could easily talk and stress something that wasn't true. Instead of keeping it on the low until they found out what occurred, he turned to face Demerea. "What does she have to do with this?" Ryan closed their small distance and looked down into her eyes. You could tell that he was trying to keep his tears from falling about the loss of Precious, but it was evident that he was hurting.

Demerea stuttered, trying to shuffle up an answer without snitching on her friend. "I-I thought—"

Ryan grabbed ahold of her arms aggressively. His lips quivered with venom. "Demerea? If you know something that I don't, I suggest you tell me right fucking now. I'm not playing with you. "

"Faith was at the party yesterday talking about Precious," she admitted.

"And?" Ryan yelled as the tears dropped slowly from the creases of his eyes.

"She was talking about ending whatever you two had going on. I tried to calm her down, but she left." Demerea was nearly on the verge of tears herself.

"Ryan, you gotta calm down," DJ whispered into his ear before grabbing him. "The police still right here, fool."

"Excuse me?" Detective Ross stepped in the middle. "I know this may be kind of hard for you right now. I'm not sure if she was your girlfriend or relative, but we're trying our best to find out what happened here last night, and if she could help us, there might be a slight chance of us solving this to give you some closure, sir. Is your name Royal?"

Ryan mugged him with suspicion. "Yeah. How do you know that?"

"Because mostly everything inside of her purse has your name written on it. Documents, club license, other miscellaneous papers. It's the reason we're searching your home right now. The neighbors said that they saw a figure that resembled a female wearing a black hoodie and blue jeans. There was a small struggle, and a gunshot that followed after," Detective Ross stated.

Ryan placed his face down into his hands and let out a horrified scream. The thought of his meeting tomorrow with Precious's uncle Lucci placed a hard ball in his court. How could you tell a man on a second meet-up for business that his niece, who introduced them, was shot in front of his home, and he didn't have a clue who was responsible just yet? The information about Faith surely had to be true, especially with the chaos she was keeping up after Ryan exposed his hand on not being with her. The pain of Precious being taken was like none other. The smell of her skin, her soft touch and kiss… She was the woman he truly wanted to gain more with, and it was snatched away because of a bitch who wanted to cause him pain and drama.

"If you guys don't mind, I'm gonna have you two wait here while I speak with this young lady alone. We don't want to flame up the situation harder than it is, and I don't need any one of you making yourself a suspect for saying something that doesn't make sense. If we can come to an understanding with her, maybe a few things will start to make sense and I will be able to clear the Philadelphia police out of your home," Ross offered.

"Whatever, man!" Ryan paced around in a small circle.

Demerea looked back into Ryan's eyes as the detective led her over to another section of officers. She knew that his mind wouldn't be able to handle another bid for this mishap, and she was not about to see herself get mixed up in any of the drama that had been occurring. It didn't take long for her to pour out the entire story she knew and give the authorities a small amount of information that could help them.

Ryan eventually moved across the street, where he spotted Nas posted in front of his neighbor's apartment. DJ followed closely behind until they reached the other side, where he embraced them both.

"I'm sorry, Ryan. I know this shit gotta be hard for you, homie. I know the new li'l shorty was rocking with your touch." Nas placed a hand over his heart out of respect.

Ryan wiped his face with a stern nod. "How long have you been out here?"

"For about six hours, bro. I pulled over here to snatch my re-up so I can slide out on the west side, and this is what I ran into." He motioned towards all the Philly police cruisers. "This ain't Delaware, Ryan. You might need to relocate. If somebody making shots like this to get yo' people touched, it gotta be some bad blood out in the streets."

"What do you mean bad blood? Don't nobody know I stay out here, Nas. Nobody but the niggas who in the loop with us, anyway. So what are you saying?" Ryan looked him up and down.

"Chill, Ryan. I'm saying that everybody is stressing that your baby mom popped shorty. Now I don't know how true it is, but you know how the hood talk."

"That's the second person that said Faith, bro." DJ looked at Ryan with a raised eyebrow. "It ain't no coincidence that people mention her name for wanting to hurt Precious when she was so mad at you. I've known Faith for a long time, bro, and I know that she can definitely catch a terrible attitude problem when she's in her feelings. You might need to call her and check the temperature," he suggested.

Ryan agreed with a nod and pulled his cell phone out. He scrolled through his call log until he reached Faith's name. He dialed her number while tapping his foot lightly. The line rang six times before going straight to voicemail. Trying again, he received the same action and placed the phone back into his pocket. "She's not answering. I'ma just pull up and check this bitch." Ryan started to let the anger rise again.

Before he could walk off, DJ grabbed his arm. "Don't do that, bro. You don't want your name coming up in the mix of this, period. Especially if Faith really has something to do with this. Any small interaction will place you in the same boat as her. I think you need to wait it out, bro. Just give it a day or two and if we haven't heard anything from her, you'll know," he warned.

Ryan exhaled and took a seat on the curb. DJ was right. He didn't want anyone thinking that he had anything to do with Precious being murdered, not to mention their recent business deals with the club and the clothing store she had just established. In the eyes of the authorities, it would look like a clear set-up. That was the only thing the cops could see when there was money involved.

Ryan watched the detectives grill Demerea. Ryan placed the situation in the center of his heart. If Faith had anything to do with Precious being taken away, he was gonna be sure to remove everything she ever loved away from the earth, starting with her mom and Markie-D. That was a fucking promise.

Chris Green

Chapter 2
Faith's house

Sitting up in her bed, Faith grabbed the side of her head from the massive pain that began to erupt through it. The drowsy feeling she was experiencing last night still hadn't worn off. It was now the next morning, and she was still in the same predicament.

"Ma?" she yelled out while taking a few deep breaths.

After she didn't receive a response, she slung her feet over the bed until they reached the floor. As she stood up, the sound of Prince crying erupted like an oven top overheating a tea kettle. Sighing with disbelief, Faith yelled her mother's name again. There was no way that Prince wanted to crank up just as she climbed out of the bed. His ass was bound for a nursery sooner or later, because dealing with all his damn hollering and a terrible headache wasn't about to mix at all.

As she stepped out into the hallway, the sound of an officer yelling caused Faith to jump out of her damn skin.

"Get the fuck on the ground! Get on the ground or I'll shoot!"

Faith looked over as a huge man in a bulletproof vest climbed the small steps with his gun pointed. Faith did as she was told and got on the floor. Within seconds, the officer was placing her into a pair of handcuffs as a few detectives started to move past her into the bedrooms.

"What the hell is going on?" Faith yelled in fear. The sound of Prince continuing to cry caused her to jerk under the bulky officer. "What's wrong with my son? Can someone please tell me what the fuck is going on?"

"Ma'am, calm down. Your son is fine," he replied before lifting her from the carpeted floor.

"Why am I in handcuffs? I haven't done shit," she questioned with her head moving back and forth like a ratchet junkie from the block.

The officer continued to move her down the stairs where her mother stood with Prince crying in her arms.

"Ma, what are these people doing? Why am I in handcuffs?"

"What did you do, Faith?" Ms. Anderson gave her a disappointed frown. "I warned you."

"Ma, I didn't do anything. What are you talking about?"

Police were flooding the house by the second, and her mama refused to fill her in on what was going on. Her warm motherly love wasn't there, judging from the nasty look plastered on her face, and every time Faith tried to speak with her, she tooted her nose and turned in the opposite direction.

Detective Ross stepped through the threshold of their home and smiled once he spotted Faith in cuffs. Moving over to her mother, he rubbed Ms. Anderson's shoulders gently as if he was consoling her for whatever reason. Right after, he made his way towards Faith and his gentle, supporting face was now out the window.

"Faith Anderson, my name is Detective Ross. Can you tell me your whereabouts from around ten to eleven-thirty last night?" he questioned with a straight face.

"What?" She looked over at her mother with a confused face.

"Just answer the question, Faith!" Ms. Anderson snapped.

"I was here. I came from my friend's party and crashed out because I had a headache. What the hell is going on?"

"Sir, we found it." The officer who trailed down the stairs of their home held a black bag in his hands towards Detective Ross.

Faith watched as he grabbed the bag and pulled a .380 automatic pistol from inside. The black hoodie was next. "Would you happen to know who this belongs to, Faith?" he asked with a suspicious grin.

"Yes. The gun is mine. My dad gave it to me for my seventeenth birthday. That's not my hoodie. I've never seen it before. Can someone please tell me what's going on?"

Detective Ross placed all the evidence into a large plastic bag and closed the space between them. "Last night, a woman by the name of Precious Edmond was murdered, and your name has been mentioned in connection to the crime," he confirmed.

"What? Murder? I haven't killed anyone. I don't even know this girl. This has to be a mistake," Faith panicked.

"No, it's not a mistake, and I'm sure that this gun will be the evidence coinciding with what the authorities are expecting. Your friend Demerea Watson told us about the recent episode at her home last night, about the way you wanted to end what she and Mr. Royal had going on, that she wouldn't live to see it prosper with him. Or maybe that's just a figment of her imagination?" Detective Ross questioned, folding his arms.

Hearing that Demerea had spilled their conversation to the police was mad lame, but still, it would never cross her mind to actually murder Precious just because of Ryan being a dirty-ass nigga. Faith may have pondered beating her ass a few times, but never doing something so stupid that would drag her away from Prince. She glanced over at her mother with worry. She dropped a few tears before speaking. "Mama, these people have a misconception of me. You know that I wouldn't do that."

Ms. Anderson looked at her daughter's face, and she wanted to believe her so badly. The turmoil with Ryan was a problem she had warned Faith about months ago, and now the shit was exploding in her face. "You made your bed, Faith. Now you gotta lay in it," she said while rocking Prince in her arms

"Mama, I ain't do shit!" Faith started to cry harder.

"Faith Anderson. You're under arrest for the murder of Precious Edmond. Anything you say can and will be used against you in a court of law. You have the right to a legal representative. If you can't afford one, there will be one appointed to you. Is there anything else you would like to say to me or your mom before you leave?" Detective Ross grabbed her handcuffed wrist.

"I didn't touch that girl. I was drunk last night and came home to get in the bed. That's it. I swear. "Faith looked back and forth between him and her mother.

"I'm sorry, Faith. As much as I want to believe you, my hands are tied. I have to take you in and let the judge make a ruling on that." Detective Ross escorted her towards the front door.

"Mama, I didn't do it! Why are you letting these people do this? My dad can vouch for me, sir. He's at work. Just get him on the phone, please! I can't leave my son!" Faith kicked violently as she was removed from the home and placed inside the back of a police cruiser.

* * *

Ryan's spot, two hours later

"I can't believe this shit." Ryan sat on his couch watching the news speaking about Precious's death. Just the feeling of sitting in his home caused his skin to crawl, knowing that she had been murdered in front of his door. A picture of Faith continued to flash across the screen, and nothing could stop his heart from hating her fucking guts. Precious was not only his future wife, but a friend that could never be replaced by anyone who walked the earth. She was his guide to a better future, and no one he ever encountered had the mindframe that she possessed. That strong love and genuine support was now gone, and Faith was the shiesty-ass bitch to thank. "She really pulled this grimy-ass shit. I'm just lost for words right now." Ryan's hands rubbed across his face in exhaustion.

DJ sat at Ryan's kitchen table with a hand under his chin. Something just wasn't sitting right, but he just couldn't put his finger on it. Faith wasn't only a hot head; she was smart. She would never tarnish Prince's life, especially when you had a crazy nigga for a baby daddy like Ryan.

Demerea wasn't feeling the vibe, and neither was Nas. There was nothing like losing a life. There was always a bad aura left around after witnessing whatever travesty awaited your eyes.

Nas was the first one to break the awkward silence. He was trying to spread some real love around that muthafucka 'cause shit was definitely on edge inside those four walls.

"I know it's uneasy for you right now, bro, but Faith doing that should be the reason you snatch yo' little king up and make sure their side of the family is completely away from him. That would have to be your new start, as a successful black father, because you've come too far to go back."

"I don't care about none of that shit, nigga. I want Precious back. That bitch Faith's mama is not about to let me take Prince anywhere. She's been against me since day one, and she's probably blaming this shit on me right now. How in the hell am I supposed to tell this shit to her parents?"

Nas knew that was a question he couldn't answer, but he refused to quit. "That's a time that still has to come whether you want it to or not, bro. All I'm saying is have things in order with your business if things start looking shaky. People have a tendency to talk after hurtful shit like this happens, especially if they feel it's your fault like you just said. Run your bread up and just relocate, bro. It's time."

Demerea smacked her lips. "He can't just up and leave. What about everybody who still here, the ones who he loves? We play a part in that also. I can understand running up his money, but Faith did some foul shit. He needs to make sure this girl gets what she deserves about that shit. This shit got my skin itching right now, and it's not even my family." She frowned with a disgusted look.

DJ stood up from the table, shaking his head. "Can y'all just chill out for a second? 'Cause all this gonna do is make him think too quick. Yes, what's going on right now is very bad, and we have to really look and see what the hell is going on, because all this shit ain't looking right through the binoculars. Look, Faith ain't about to just spazz out and kill someone, Ryan. She's got a bad attitude problem maybe, but not enough to commit murder. Take your time with this shit, 'cause I'm telling you, it's more to this story. Regardless of what we say, you have to make your own decision about how we proceed from here, because shit is about to get extremely hot."

Ryan sat quietly for a few more seconds before rising from the couch. "I have to get rid of this last shipment, and then it's over. I'm done. I don't wanna hustle; I don't wanna be in the streets. I'm about to take my money and fight to get my son from the bitch's mama. After that, I'm going to get Kimyetta and leave up top for good. I have a meeting with these people soon, and I need to make sure this shit is accounted for. In order to do that, I gotta issue out the rest of this product," Ryan clarified.

So what are you about to do now?" DJ questioned. He was surprised to hear his friend say that the streets were something he didn't want to be a part of anymore. Ryan was a young menace causing all types of pandemonium throughout Wilmington, and now those tables had finally turned. Losing this girl actually had his heart ready to form a complete change.

"I have to meet up with everybody and make sure they're on point for this next round. Tomorrow, me and Precious were supposed to head up to Brooklyn for a deal with her uncle Lucci. I'm not sure how that's gonna turn out, so I'll need a few of y'all on standby just in case shit get ugly. It's hard to try and sell him anything when I have to explain that his niece was murdered."

"You might need to leave the part out about how you know who did it, just for safety precautions. I understand that you a real one, but I don't need you forcing yourself into a bad situation."

Ryan shrugged his shoulders. "It is what it is, DJ. I really love Precious. I'll keep it real and let it continue however he wanna take it. Regardless, Faith is not getting away with this. I'll make sure I do whatever I got to in order to see her get it in the worst way behind those walls. This shit can never be forgiven," Ryan said while grabbing his jacket.

"So what do you want us to do now?" Nas asked with impatience.

"Me and DJ gotta slide out to the east side and holla at my cousin. Once we leave there, I'll come back and break you off whatever you need. You and Demerea can just wait here until we get back. I don't wanna just leave this shit unattended."

"Why the hell you wanna leave us here alone if you know the police could be knocking on your door at any second, Ryan? What we supposed to do then?" Demerea looked at him with a serious ass face. "I'm not tryna be interrogated by those assholes no more."

"It's easy: don't open the door, and stay quiet until they leave. I'm not gonna be gone forever. Just give me time to disperse this shit, and I'll be right back." Ryan left out the front door with DJ beside him.

"Ryan?" DJ called out before they could reach the bottom of the steps.

"Wassup, bro?" He looked back up at his friend, who was stuck in the center of the stairs while pointing his finger out to the parking lot.

Following the direction he pointed, Ryan spotted the Midnight Cartel killers themselves. Summer and Winter were posted against a white Range Rover dressed in black cat suits. Their red wigs were styled differently, but the two pretty caramel faces could never be forgotten. The pistols that dangled in their palms caused Ryan to slightly freeze. He didn't know if it was a hit or maybe just a check-up from Richard, but the approach surely had the boys on edge.

"Who the fuck are they, and why in the hell are they staring at us?" DJ questioned while reaching for his pistol.

Ryan stopped him and continued to stroll towards the car. "They work for the man at the table. I don't know how in the fuck the found my crib though. Don't do anything dumb. Just act normal and get in the car."

"Act normal? Nigga, it's two bitches dressed up like Charlie's Angels in your parking lot with guns. How the hell am I supposed to act normal? What if they start shooting?" DJ whispered as they reached Ryan's Infiniti truck.

"Then shoot back, man." Before Ryan could climb in the front seat, he looked back at the girls and received a wink from Summer. The only difference between the women was a small beauty mark that rested on Winter's cheekbone. Their demeanor was the same, and the taste for blood was surely equal between them. Not sure how to respond back, Ryan nodded his head and climbed inside the truck, being sure to adjust his rearview mirror. He started the engine and pulled out of the parking lot. Both of the women stood still as a painting while his vehicle drove smoothly past them. Their eyes connected, and Ryan could tell that their mind wasn't on fucking and sucking his shoes off. They seemed to be more on a mission of blowing his ass away, and he damn sure wouldn't be slipping if that was the case.

Instead of them shooting up his truck, they let him leave the parking lot without lifting a finger. If they came to handle any business, it would've surely been taken care of immediately. That gave him the confirmation that Richard was obviously watching.

DJ looked behind them to ensure that no one was following Ryan's truck before he spoke. "Listen, bro, this shit is getting too serious out here. You got people stalking you and shit. Precious is gone. Maybe you should just say fuck it and leave, Ryan." His tone showed the fear of what was yet to come.

"I ain't going nowhere yet. I got shit to handle, and I need my son. Don't you understand that Precious is the reason I have any of this shit going on? If it wasn't for her, there would be no club, no clothing store, no Lucci Bruno. She helped me build this shit up from the ground, and it was all just snatched away. What the hell can I say to her parents in the future if I run? Well, I'm sorry, Mr. and Mrs. Edmond, but your daughter died at the hands of my slime-ass child's mother so I couldn't face you guys. I'm sure you should have gotten over it now being that a few years have gone by!" Ryan yelled with anger.

"Bro, calm down. I'm only trying to help." DJ shook his head.

"Well, help me by following my lead, DJ. Right now, that's all I need you to do. After all this is over, I won't have a reason to look back at these dirty-ass streets of Delaware again."

"Cool, bro. I won't say nothing else." DJ faced the window calmly.

Nothing could equal up to the amount of pressure that was about to fall upon Ryan's head, and DJ knew that for sure. The police were getting closer to smashing his operation from all the hoe-ass issues going on, and that shit was definitely not about to hinder DJ from going to college, period. Before he squandered his scholarship over a few bad decisions, he would turn his back and let Ryan handle the drama on his own.

After a silent ride to the east side, Ryan pulled down Torey's block and parked directly in front of his spot. The crowd of men who stood posted out front paused their conversation when they spotted him, and DJ stepped out of the truck.

"Well if it ain't Mr. Big Money," Free teased after realizing who it was.

Trying not to feed off his pussy-ass energy, Ryan continued to walk up the driveway.

"The nigga must have lost his bitch or something. He usually have somethin' to say." Free laughed.

Turning quickly on his heels, Ryan rushed over to him and placed a solid punch to his nose. The hard fist sent him to the ground, and the pistol from his hip followed up, pressing down on Free's forehead aggressively

The other men who stood around pulled their guns, aiming for Ryan's head, until DJ jumped in the center of them. "Wait! Everybody calm down. Let's just wait for a second."

"Fuck that, DJ. Move!" Ryan barked. "I'm ready to do this shit. Y'all niggas think I'm something to fucking play with around here, huh?" He pressed his gun into Free's face while the other men scrambled around nervously.

"Ryan, please chill," DJ begged, still holding out his hands in front of all the weapons.

Torey rushed from the house with his gun in hand and made his way over to the confrontation. "What the fuck is going on?" His face looked like he was ready to spill a nigga's head wide open.

"This nigga's mouth, bro. I'm tired of it. He popping like shit is sweet. I'll kill you in front of all these niggas, boy." Ryan looked down in Free's face with demon-like eyes.

"Fuck you, nigga! Pull that bitch!" Free bucked, not wanting to lose any stripes in front of his entourage.

"Cuzzo, I don't know what's going on, but you killing him right here ain't gonna end too well. Let him go. Come in the house, and let's talk." Torey tapped Ryan's shoulder with a stern look.

Exhaling deeply, Ryan lowered his gun and stepped back so Free's bitch ass could get to his feet.

"You dead, nigga. That's a promise." Free smiled, wiping the blood from his nose.

"Watch yo' fucking mouth and take a walk or somethin', nigga. I warned you about your mouth. If y'all niggas wanna meet up later on for a one on one, we can do that. Business comes before all that shit, so take a walk." Torey pointed at Free and the rest of his crew.

Torey tapped Ryan on his chest, gesturing for him to follow. Torey walked smoothly back up the driveway and stepped inside of his spot. After Ryan and DJ crossed the threshold, he locked the screen door and took a seat back at his kitchen table.

"Look, Ryan, you can't be coming over here getting into with my people, man. I stand on this Eastside shit the same way you stand on the north. That shit makes me look bad, and the only reason you ain't die in front of that yard is because you my fucking cousin. What the hell is going on with you?" He sparked a Newport, sitting back.

Ryan rubbed the bridge of his nose and took a seat while DJ remained standing. "I got a lot going on right now."

"That I already know. You made the news, idiot. You got females killing each other and shit. Wassup with that?"

"None of your concern."

"It's my concern if you doing business with me, Ryan. I don't need no hot shit around here on my block. My name is in too much already to have the police creeping anywhere around me!" Torey snapped.

"I just told you I got it under control, nigga. I got a shipment for you in the truck, but this is it. After this, I'm leaving the state. I'm going down south for a while until shit dies down. It's more than five though," Ryan gave him the heads up.

"What do you mean it's more than five?"

"I gotta double you up because I'm running short on motherfuckers I trust. I'm on a timescale to get this shit off, and I know you can handle this shit more discreetly than anyone I'm dealing with. Take your thirty off the top, and I'll collect the rest within a week. Do you think you can make that shake?"

"I guess I ain't got no option if you *telling* me instead of asking, genius." Torey tossed his cigarette filter in the ashtray.

"DJ, can you grab that for me?" Ryan nodded.

Following instructions without giving a response, DJ headed out the front door to retrieve the package. Ryan waited until he closed the door behind him to speak.

"Look, Torey, that was my baby mama who did that to my li'l shorty. I don't know what the reason was, but I know the police is asking questions. There's no reason for you to think that the Feds gonna come kick in yo' shit, but that ain't gonna mean that I'm not gonna need your help if trouble comes my way. I know we haven't gained too much of a bond growing up, but you're still family no matter what."

"Save the sob story, nigga. As long as you ain't doing nothing to harm me, I'm beside you, period. All I ask is that you don't lead any of that fuckery my way. I got a mission of my own too, Ryan."

"That's understood. I'm not worried about doing that, because I'm keeping shit tighter than tight."

Ryan's eyes cut back to DJ walking through the front door. He moved smoothly over to Torey and placed the bag on his kitchen table. "Like I said, we gonna be good. If you can make this happen for me, I got an idea on a better way to make some cheese legitimately." Ryan winked over at his cousin before standing from the couch.

Torey flashed a half-smile with a nod. "It's your world. I'm just Mr. Ramirez looking for a way to Puerto Rico."

"I see you been practicing your lines for comedy school, nigga." Ryan grinned before shaking his hand.

Leaving through the front door, Ryan and DJ headed back down to the truck. The small crew of men posted up on the lawn as if they were itching to hear one remark. Free mugged Ryan until he climbed behind the driver's seat of his Infiniti. Instead of making a comment, he slowly pulled away from his cousin's crib.

"So do you think he's gonna keep it one hunnid with the keys? I mean, I know you gave him five before, but this is double. The last time he was a few big dollars short after that recount." DJ stared out of the window as if he was just making small talk.

"I ain't got no choice. He was able to move it, and that's what I need right now. After I make this money, I'm cashing in and getting the hell away from this city.

It's easy," Ryan replied while turning off the secluded street.

"So what's your plan for tomorrow? Because there's no way Lucci Bruno is about to buy thirty bricks from you after he finds out that his niece was murdered. Do you think it's safe to trust that on top of what you already have on your plate?"

"Who knows, DJ? I ain't got no other way then these same resources, unless you see something better than this. The more people we add, the more baggage we bring, bro. I'm trying to keep it under the radar for us to get around these people. One slip, and all of us could be in danger."

"I'm not trying to make you angry, bro. I'm just trying to get you to think. It's a lot going on, really too much for you to handle. Maybe you need to just split and grab Kimyetta and Prince. Once you get settled, you can send for them." DJ was trying to give him some good advice before shit spiraled more out of control.

Instead of answering him, Ryan headed straight for DJ's block. It didn't take longer than ten minutes, and truthfully, Ryan didn't want to hear anything else about failing when he had already lost so much. The thought of Precious alone made him want to drop a tear, and that was the same reason he needed some time alone to think.

Pulling up in front of his friend's home, Ryan slowed down his truck and looked over at DJ. "Early tomorrow morning I'm heading to Brooklyn. I gotta see where this goes with Lucci. If you're with it, be at the crib around seven a.m."

Shaking his head, DJ opened the door and stepped out. "Be careful, Ryan," he mumbled before closing the truck door behind him. His facial expression alone told Ryan that he could surely count him out.

"Always," he replied before swerving back off into the street.

With or without anyone, Ryan was gonna be sure to show his face down every avenue before making his exit. The same hood he fed was ready to crumble down on him, and he damn sure wasn't about to be a statistic for the hood - even if it meant crossing motherfuckers out. That was a promise.

Chapter 3
Ryan's spot, north side of Philly

It was a little past twelve-thirty when Ryan arrived back at his crib. The sight of Demerea jumping up from his couch forced him to stop and look around. "Where the hell did Nas go?" He closed the front door while looking at her shake off the small slumber she had been in.

"Umm. He said something about he had to be in Wilmington for some business on the west side. He should be making his way back after he's done."

Ryan sat on the couch directly next to her. She gazed at him, at a loss for words. It was hard to console someone who was grieving about a death. "I know it may be hard for you, Ryan, and I damn sure can't say that I understand how you feel, because I don't. The only thing I can tell you is that I'm here if you need me to do anything. Whatever," she emphasized to let him know that she was serious. Her hand touched his knee.

Demerea was giving him that thirsty slave look, and he surely knew what she meant. "What you saying?" he asked curiously.

"I mean whatever you want me to do. I can cook for you, give you some head, pussy, whatever you tell me to do. I just wanna show you that every girl ain't foul, Ryan. I respect your hustle, and I know for a fact that you've shown everybody love without any pressure. You have to also take time to relax." Her almond-shaped eyes were glaring at him to make sure he knew that she was far from bullshitting.

Ryan roamed his pupils up and down her body with a straight face and then he exhaled. "I'm past even caring about all that, Demerea. You don't have to worry about me. Do whatever you want." He stood from the couch and headed for his room.

After stepping inside, Ryan shut the door and crashed out on the bed. The silence was looming around heavily and every second he sat still, the thought of Precious would flicker through his brain.

After lying in the same spot for over five minutes, the sound of his bedroom door cracking caused his eyes to open. The sight of Demerea standing naked in front of his bed forced him to bite his tongue. He wanted to snap so badly, but her nice-ass figure was more than just eye candy. Her titties were a nice set of B-cups. Her waist was slender, and her butt was definitely poking out for a girl her size.

"What are you doing, Demerea?" he asked as she climbed down on the bed with him.

Unbuttoning his pants, she rubbed her breasts in satisfaction and flopped his dick out into her other hand. "You told me I can do whatever I want, Ryan," she replied before wrapping her lips around him.

Moving with a slow pace, Demerea bobbed her head slowly, letting him grow inside of her mouth. After he expanded to his full length, she started to speed up, forcing him down her throat.

The wetness from her tongue game forced Ryan to cringe up and place his hand behind her head. She was taking him down like a pro, and didn't hesitate to gag if she had to. Her eyes stayed locked on him the entire time, and her amazing arch-up was so enticing. Rubbing her plump butt cheeks one by one, Ryan closed his eyes and started to push Demerea's head down harder. The slobber from her lips was rushing down, stating that she was doing the job, and Ryan didn't want to see her stop until he was satisfied. Her head continued to bounce on his meat, sucking him seductively, while he gripped a handful of her ass. Feeling that rise come from his member, he snatched it from her warm mouth and stood up. Demerea could see that he was beyond in the groove now. His shit was harder than a brick wall, and the way she was tooting that ass up forced his eyes to go crooked for a second. Easing behind her, he shoved his shit in quicker than a teen getting his virginity broken. The feeling forced Demerea to bite down on her fingers. His shit was definitely big enough to wreck some shit, and the way her pussy pooted, he was damn sho' in deep enough.

"Ssss. Slow down, Ryan." Demerea tried to match his rhythm. Her ass was rocking harder than a wave from his strokes, but that shit felt so good to her kitty.

"Shut up," he ordered. Latching on to her waist, he raised one of his legs and dropped his shit deeper than an anchor in the ocean.

"Ohhh God!" She grabbed the sheets to brace the way her shit was being punished. Demerea jumped off his manhood to catch a deep breath. "Damn, Ryan, go easy! You act like your dick still being cuffed in a Pamper, nigga." She rotated her hips back and forth slowly.

Ignoring the statement, he flipped Demerea on her back and pulled her towards him. Rubbing his cick up and down her sweet split, he dug in slowly. Her lips separated. She tried to force a moan, but it was caught inside her throat. Demerea's juices were soaking him more with every motion he took. After stabbing that pussy for a cool twenty minutes, they both released a hard-ass orgasm and collapsed down next to each other.

"Thank you." He pecked her cheek with a light smirk. "Sex doesn't make me feel better, but I do enjoy it with you."

"Oh, really? Nigga, you talking like I'm your first bought stripper or something. I give you pussy because you a real one, Ryan." Demerea smiled, slapping his back lightly.

"Nah, you know I'll never try you like that. You definitely bussin' like a professional stripper though." He chuckled.

"Mm-hmm. I can do more than that. I'm just glad to see you smile. I know this shit is mind-blowing for you, especially the way DJ making you all unsettled and shit. He acts like him and Faith still fucking or something." Demerea started to play with Ryan's dick as if the statement didn't just freeze time.

Raising up, Ryan grabbed her hand with a stern look. "What the fuck did you just say?"

"I said that DJ moving like he still fucking Faith, because of the way he keep trying to take up for her."

"Wait! What the fuck do you mean DJ fucked Faith?"

Demerea sat up next to him. Her face was inches away from his, and you could see that Ryan was truly lost about their past. "Wait, you mean to tell me that you didn't know DJ and Faith had sex before they met you? You gotta remember that you didn't move on our side until after middle school. How do you think DJ got with Rose? Whatever him and Faith tried to make happen obviously was over, so she introduced him to that bitch. That's when you came along about a year later," she exposed with a straight face. "I thought he told you this."

Ryan's fist clenched so tightly that veins began to protrude from his forehead. "That slimy-ass hoe was playing me the whole time. That's why that nigga been acting funny. Why the fuck ain't nobody ever said nothing to me!" he yelled through tight lips.

Demerea slid back a tad, seeing that he was furious. "Ryan, DJ claimed that he talked with you about that. It wasn't our place to say anything. Now Faith is even more wrong if she didn't keep shit a million with you from the jump about what they did. Everybody knew. Even Wicked and Reckless," Demerea admitted.

"I'ma kill that nigga's ass." Ryan moved to jump out of the bed, but Demerea grabbed a hold of his arm.

"Wait! Don't move so fast, Ryan. This is the same nigga that knows all yo' business, and everybody knows that y'all rock together like glue and paper. This would be the time to think smart, because all yo' shit can fall down right here if you make the wrong decision."

Her words definitely woke his ass back up to reality, because there was damn sho' tons of shit on his plate. After all the years of being friends, Ryan would've never thought that DJ would hold something so serious back from him. The vision of him on top of Faith left a bad taste in Ryan's mouth, and there was no coming back from a nasty-ass secret like that. Faith was his child's mother, but hearing the shit Demerea exposed forced him to think otherwise.

"Listen, Ryan. This may sound crazy to you, but things like this is normal when you're around a whole bunch of deceiving-ass, lying people. They held some shit from you that was supposed to have been mentioned from the jump. Now I'm not the smartest person in the world, but you're the one who's having the money right now. These other lowlifes are just hanging around waiting for a free KFC meal. If you stop, they have nothing. Handle your affairs, then make them pay for whatever after. If you need my help, I'll be here," Demerea assured him.

"And what, is that supposed to make me feel like you ain't just like them?" Ryan gave her a deadly frown. "I'm starting not to trust anybody."

"I don't need shit from you, boy. I got my own everything, and my father makes sure I'm good in every way. You were just a real nigga blinded by a dumb-ass female, and that's normal shit that you have to face in order to ensure that you jump that hurdle the next time around. You don't have to trust me or use my help. But if you need me, I'm here. That's the difference, Ryan. Others were forcing themselves to be a part of your shit. I'm just waiting to be picked and placed in the game. Only if you want me to." She massaged his dick until it stood back up in her hand. "Fuck Faith, because she's gone forever. But you have me."

Ryan leaned back on the bed as her hand slowly stroked his piece. "What's better about you?" he replied sarcastically.

Demerea climbed on top of him. She squatted over him cowgirl style, allowing her beautiful ass to be viewed, guiding him back inside her gushy walls. She eased down on his shit and looked back. "Because I'm Demerea," she answered before riding away on his manhood.

Instead of objecting, Ryan watched as her ass cheeks bounced smoothly up and down. The intoxicating feeling calmed him for a second, but it couldn't take his mind off the shit he had just heard. DJ was really a stone cold snake. A friend in disguise. Shit was still surely gonna be addressed, and however it flowed from there would be the last conversation that nigga ever had with Ryan - or with anybody else in the world if his mouth fixed up a lie.

The sound of Demerea's ass colliding with his pelvis zoned him back out. He was surely about to place her in position. From that day on, she was stamped *his* - at least until he found better.

"Bounce on that shit harder." He slammed a hand down on her ass.

"Sss. Yes, daddy," she moaned while locking back into his eyes.

Chris Green

Chapter 4
Brooklyn, New York, Pink House Projects
8:34 a.m.

After gathering all the help he could, Ryan ended up making the small trip with three people the next morning. Nas and Freddie were strapped to be sure his safety was secured. If he didn't arrive back out of the projects within twenty minutes, they were coming inside, and everyone from the outside in would catch a bullet from the fully automatic Mac-90's they carried.

Demerea sat in the passenger seat of his car and made sure to wear the tightest dress she could. Her switchblade was tucked inside her bra, and two sharp razors were tucked under her tongue just in case she had to trick a few of the clowns in front of the building.

Once Ryan pulled in front of the building, he reached for the two duffle bags in the backseat and was sure to take his gun off safety in case he needed to make a drastic move.

"Do you want me to stay in the car and wait?' Demerea asked with a curious eye.

"Only get out if you see some fishy shit. I don't need you getting hurt on no hero shit," Ryan stated before stepping out of the car with the two bags in hand.

The movement of the Crip neighborhood shifted when he placed his two feet on the pavement. The leader of the pack was standing in the center of the street with his arms folded. Boo Daddy's face was clean and mean with no sign of happiness in his system. The blue 600 MurdaBlock shirt he wore matched his fitted designer jeans, and the Glock nine positioned on his hip stated that he was definitely gonna handle that business on yo' ass if you started slippin' where they was Crippin'.

Ryan held his composure, walking smoothly across the small street. Just as he reached the other side, the men who stood next to Boo Daddy removed their guns quickly.

"Is there a problem, guys? I'm coming to see Lucci." Ryan cut his eyes at the big man in charge.

Boo Daddy stepped in front of the crew and looked Ryan in his eyes. "You must really got a death wish coming here after what just occurred?"

"I don't know what you're talking about. I'm here to see Lucci, the same as last time. Nothing else is new." Ryan kept a firm stare so Boo Daddy could know that there wasn't any fear in his bones.

"All eyes are on you, li'l homie. Be careful," he replied with a smirk before stepping out of his way.

The rest of the Crips followed the lead and allowed him to enter the project building. Of course as Ryan kept walking, he knew that any one of the gang members could blow his back out, but turning around at that point would do him no justice. It was obvious Lucci was probably aware of what had happened. After all, he was a powerful man, and Ryan knew the police had already contacted Precious's parents since they were her next of kin, so the word about Precious was surely out.

Upon entering the building, Ryan made his way to Lucci's floor and proceeded down the long hallway until he reached his door. Setting the bags on the floor, he huffed before knocking lightly. The creepy breezeway was forcing him to be on edge. There was no telling if a nigga was coming to murder him or rob him for the shit he had. In New York, it was bound to happen, and there was nothing he could do about it.

The shuffling of Lucci's door locks grabbed Ryan's attention. After a few seconds of fumbling, Lucci stuck his head out and stared at Ryan with a blank face. The silence was so thick, you could hear the birds chirping outside of the building. Without saying a word, Lucci stepped to the side, allowing him to enter. Lucci reapplied the locks and moved towards his living room couch. Taking a seat, he picked up his burning cigar and motioned towards Ryan to take a seat. His face was twitching with anger, and you could tell that he was fixing his words and thoughts before speaking.

"I'm gonna give you one chance, son. One chance to explain what the fuck happened to my niece. My beautiful flower is dead, and I had to hear this from my sister over the phone early this morning. Please. I would like to know." Lucci crossed one leg over the other as if he was about to listen to a bedtime story. His eyes were dark red and there was definitely a negative aura floating throughout his apartment.

Ryan cleared his throat before speaking. "Lucci, I'm still searching throughout the streets to find out who did this. Precious was someone dear to me. Not just because she was your niece. She was also my friend. That's the reason I'm sitting here in your home now. I'm in need of answers, and I'm not gonna stop until I find them," Ryan stated with a stern tone.

"And what makes you think that I believe that, Ryan? Do you think that I live in these projects because they are cheap? Or maybe I do it for protection? That's not the case, kid. I'm here because the obvious is always the easiest way to win, son. With that being said, I know that there's more to your story." Lucci Bruno placed his cigar back in the ashtray and leaned forward. "The kilos you sold me. They came from Delaware. There was a stamping on the package when you gave it to me, Ryan. A small R was engraved at the top corner of every brick. There's only one person I know who has that stamp, kid."

Ryan looked him in the eyes, not knowing where the conversation was going. "What do you mean?

"I mean you're dealing with Richard and the Midnight Cartel. Does that ring any bells, since you seem to have lost your memory?"

Ryan's wondered how the fuck Lucci Bruno knew anything about Richard. His posture was extremely calm, but Lucci could see the worry spilling directly through his pores. "How did you know that?"

"Because Richard is on the shit list of a lot of people. Men like the one standing behind you. "

Ryan slowly turned his head and touched the barrel of a Carbon 15 assault rifle. The man who was holding the gun held a firm finger on the trigger as if he was ready to pull it. A long scar ran from the top of his right eye down to the center of his neck, and his appearance stated that his money was longer than that of the average young stupid hustler on the block. He sported a black Giovanni collared shirt with a pair of white Balmain jeans. A black Oakland Raiders snapback was lowered down over his eyes, and the loafers on his feet cost over two grand easily. The only thing that didn't cost a penny was the death-struck look in his eyes. It even caused Ryan's heart to race quickly, not knowing if the smooth-ass nigga was about to pull the trigger.

Lucci cleared his throat before lighting a cigarette. "Ryan, I'd like you to meet Ghost. He's a close friend of mine, and it seems that you have something he's interested in. The situation with my niece will be another problem on your hands, but I'm gonna allow him to handle the show for now with this issue. I would suggest that you form whatever story you have now, because he has questions."

"What the fuck do you want with me? I ain't got nothing for you, unless you're trying to buy the rest of my supply," Ryan replied as if the killer in front of him didn't ruffle his feathers.

"First of all, shut the fuck up before I blow your brains onto Lucci's coffee table. I'm not sure what you think you know, or who the fuck you think you are, but I'll explain a little bit about me so we can have an understanding. I'll murder your entire family down to the fucking pets if you feel like I'm a fucking joke. I'm a nightmare for kitten-ass niggas like you, and I'm here to offer you an opportunity instead of just emptying yo' shit right now. Now would be the time to reply, li'l man." Ghost racked the chamber of the gun back quicker than the blink of an eye.

Ryan's pride wanted to buck, but he could feel that the situation was surely not a test. "I understand, bro."

"Good. If you can tell me a few things and lead me in the right direction, I'll make it worth your while. That little-ass dope you selling can't compare to the money I can place in your pocket."

"What the fuck do you want from me, man?"

Ghost walked from behind Ryan and moved over to Lucci's side. "I wanna ask you about the people you moving this dope for. Do you know who they are?"

"Obviously. Lucci just told you, bro. The motherfucker's name is Richard." Ryan's foot rocked nervously. He wanted to reach for the gun on his hip, but something said that shit wasn't gonna end the correct way if he pulled that stunt.

"That's not what I mean. Do you really know the history of the motherfuckers you're dealing with? The ones who sit at that little table with you?"

"We all sell drugs. What else is there to know?" Ryan shrugged his shoulders

"Okay, from this day on, since you don't know who the fuck you're moving bricks across Delaware for, you work for me. Please allow me to know if you're thinking of bucking because I will find you and eat yo' fucking face like a shrimp platter." Ghost took a seat next to him and pulled out a wad of pictures. "Is this Richard?" He pointed out the first photo.

Ryan studied the man and knew without a doubt that it was definitely the Midnight Cartel leader. "Yeah, that's him."

"If you don't mind me asking, kid, how long have you been slaving for these people without knowing who the fuck they really are?" Lucci butted in.

"I've only done two runs. What's the big deal? What does this have to do with anything? I brought the supply. It's pure and uncut. Where's all this extra stuff coming from?"

"Ryan, Richard is a cop, and so is everyone else who's working anywhere around that table." Lucci smirked. The look on his face told Ryan that he was definitely not bullshitting.

"What?"

"You heard me clearly, kid. You've been dealing weight for the police. Richard is a lieutenant for the Delaware police force. Back in the nineties, I ran across his table through a mutual friend. It wasn't hard for me to see that these motherfuckers were crooked and involved with some other shit. What white male can you name me dealing smack in one if the roughest cities and no one knows of this guy? I found out the hard way after he made an appearance to my first court date when I became Delaware's most wanted. The Midnight Cartel is a table full of crooked cops, besides the few who are oblivious to what's going on like you. The process is easy. They're cops by day and criminals by night. The product you're receiving is taken straight out of evidence and placed into Richard's hands. He dishes it out to you guys, and after you make the quota of what he needs, he relieves you of your seat. Correct?" Lucci questioned.

Ryan nodded his head, but continued to listen. The information that was being laid on him was critical. After getting in the mix with Bradley, things should have been clear. There was a reason they chose Ryan - the same reason he removed Cheek Raw from the streets. He needed to be sure his mouth remained closed from the same shit that was being revealed at that exact moment.

"So now that you know you're dealing with the fucking cops. You know that there are only a few more runs before these people knock yo' shit loose. I'm here to try and prevent that by getting your help. If you decide to oblige, there's two million dollars in it for you. If you don't want to, me and Lucci could give it to the Crips outside of the building and let them decide where they gonna dump you off at. Including the bitch and two niggas you came with." Ghost shrugged with a raised eyebrow.

The sound of two million dollars nearly made Ryan's balls shrivel. That was a big-ass number for a motherfucker claiming to need his help for anything. Scrambling for a hundred thousand around Delaware could get the average nigga wasted, so an opportunity for two mil sounded way too good for Ryan to believe. "You wanna give me two million dollars to help you?"

"That's what the fuck I just said. It's plenty more where that came from, depending on how much you know and how quick you can find out. "

Ryan learned forward with anticipation. The wishy-washy feeling from earlier was cleared away, and he was now all ears to what the older killer had to say. Money like that wasn't being run across unless you were willing to do some foul shit, so if he was speaking good, Ryan was damn sho' about to be on board. "What exactly do you want me to do?

"First, I wanna know everything you know about the current table. The people. The location. The description. Then I wanna know if you met the real boss over Richard?" Ghost asked sternly.

"I'm confused. What do you mean real boss? I thought Richard was in charge."

"No. He's only the face. Have you ever heard him mention a woman's name?"

Ryan took a second to think thoroughly, especially since there was two million dollars on the line. After pondering for a few seconds, a famous line of Richard's crossed his mind. "I've never seen anyone, but he's always mentioning something about the boss lady not being happy if anybody fucked up the numbers. That's all."

Ghost glanced over to Lucci Bruno and smiled, before looking back at Ryan. "Have you ever heard him mention a woman by the name of Eva?"

"Eva? I don't think so."

"I'm sure that you will soon. Your new mission is simple, young'un. Attend the meetings as if all is normal. I need to know if the name Eva is mentioned. I need to know if she is seen just one time. After you get me all the details and confirm that you've seen her with your own eyes, I can handle the rest from there. You'll receive your money, and I'll handle any further issues that you have with Richard. The main goal is Eva. Can you remember that?" Ghost questioned again to be sure that he understood.

"Yeah, I understand. But what am I supposed to do about the supply? I can't show up to the meeting without the money." Ryan looked back and forth between both men.

Ghost moved to the side of Lucci's entertainment center and grabbed a large Nike tote bag. After dropping it at Ryan's feet, he stepped back. "I would like to take the time to let you know that this situation is bigger than you, but I'm not with the whole gay-ass mushy shit. Handle yo' business and you get paid. It's quite simple." He nodded down to the sack full of money.

Standing to his feet, Ryan tossed the bag across his back and glanced over at Lucci. The Italian's face expressed that he was still salty about the news of Precious, but the nigga Ghost was obviously in charge. "How am I supposed to keep y'all on game with what's going on?"

"Let me worry about that. I'll find you, li'l nigga." Ghost's voice was positive, and his eyes said that he would make sure of it.

Not sure how to take that answer, Ryan opened the door and left Lucci Bruno's home. After he stepped into the filthy hallway of the Pink House Projects, he exhaled a sigh of relief. Being sure not to take any risky chances, Ryan pulled out his gun and moved swiftly down the corridor until he reached the flight of stairs leading to the first floor. After making his way down, he exited the building and was sure to keep his eyes trained on his car.

Demerea was sitting slightly on the hood as if she was just seconds from coming in to get him her damn self. The gang members gazed at him suspiciously, but he didn't bite the bait. Walking through the large crowd, he made it across the street. Demerea stood up straight with her arms folded.

"Are you okay? We thought something happened to you, Ryan. I was about to slice every pussy motherfucker standing in front of this bitch if you got touched," she lied.

"I'm fine. Hurry up and get in the car - now," he stressed while climbing in the driver's seat. After she jumped her ass back on the passenger side, Ryan didn't waste any time smashing off.

When he reached the end of the street, Ryan honked his horn at Nas and Freddie, who waited in their rental. Nas placed a thumb out of the window and bent a quick U-turn in the street to follow him out of the Brooklyn neighborhood.

"Are you sure you're okay, Ryan?" Demerea asked, peeping how tense he was.

"Not really, but it doesn't even matter anymore. There's a whole new objective, and if we can make this happen, I'll be able to make sure all of y'all can live good for a long-ass time. Just let us get back to Delaware," he stressed, looking back and forth in his rearview mirror.

Ghost's words had him paranoid. It was creepy as fuck when you didn't know a motherfucker was watching you from a distance, not to mention that motherfucker was a cold-blooded killer. The aura he got from the recent situation was definitely one that he never wanted to experience again, but the news of his little police-ass friends was even more shocking. It was time to lay all the pieces down in order because now shit was about to crumble, and he damn sure wasn't about to be the one it landed it on.

Richard was in for a treat. A real Midnight Cartel special.

Chris Green

Chapter 5

After spending an entire night in a crowded women's tank, Faith was booked in the Wilmington precinct for first degree murder. The disgusting sack lunches they tried to feed her were thrown back up after one bite, and the horrible smell of the homeless ladies in the cell was biting harder than forty flies on a bowl of shit. Stepping out for a night of fun had turned out horribly. Getting drunk was surely memorable, but murdering Precious damn sure wasn't in her recollection. Regardless of how much she hated the preppy-ass bitch, she never would've crossed the line to do something so stupid. After placing a phone call to her dad Markie-D the night before, he assured her that he was going to hire her a lawyer with whatever money he possessed. She even tried calling Ryan's phone to stress her innocence, but the call was rejected every time.

It was like him to be foolish thinking that she pulled some bullshit like shooting his little girlfriend after all the motherfuckers this nigga killed throughout Delaware. It was even sadder for their son Prince, who was stuck with the same bitch that she felt wouldn't turn on her for anybody. After all the fake-ass mommy speeches Ms. Anderson was giving, her father Markie D exposed that she called the cops after spotting her daughter come in the middle of the night intoxicated with a gun. It was more than suspicious, and the fingers were pointing all types of ways after the drama unfolded throughout the night.

Out of everyone who could've told. Her mother snatched up ten thousand dollars to see her daughter be carried away on a murder that she didn't even commit.

The female officer who escorted her through the halls made a quick stop at medical to have her blood drawn before she was taken up to a pod. The sight of Wicked sitting in the small room forced her heart to race slowly. It had been so long since she had spoken to him, and the look on his face wasn't happy to see her at all.

"Wicked, oh my God! Have you been okay?"

The male officer with him stood a few feet away from his chair as if he was one of the troublemaking inmates. His eyes fluttered a few times before he cracked an evil smile.

"Wouldn't you like to know, Faith? I'm sure Ryan knows, being that he had my fucking cousin killed." His voice was low and thick.

"What? Wicked, what are you talking about?" Reckless was killed in front of the precinct. That had nothing to do with Ryan."

"Oh yeah? Not according to the word on the street. Free from the east side claims that Ryan paid him to handle a mission for him and didn't know it was Reckless until the smoke was clear. He set my fucking cousin up," Wicked mumbled in a lower voice after the officer cut his eyes over to them.

"Hey! No talking to the women, big guy." The white man lifted Wicked out of his spot to seat him outside on the hallway bench.

"Get the fuck off me, cracker!" Wicked barked loudly.

"Easy, big guy. I'm only following protocol. Let's make it to the hallway - now!"

As Wicked walked past Faith, he whispered the words clearly to her face. "I'm gonna kill every last one of y'all when they let me out of this place in a few months. Get lost while you got the chance."

The female officer lowered her head as if he was talking to her scary ass.

The shit Wicked was spitting from his lips didn't sound right. Reckless and Ryan were friends regardless of whatever small disagreements they went through. Ryan was crazy, but he wasn't fucking stupid. Dealing with her baby daddy was a death wish. He only wanted to live up to Raekwon's name, and that's what forced everyone to build their fake-ass hatred for him as if he was the one killing his own friends. Wicked's threat fell on deaf ears, because if he got out playing with Ryan in any kind of way, he was sure to die wherever he stood.

"Anderson." The small black nurse called Faith's name, breaking her thought process.

After taking a tube full of her blood for testing, the female officer escorted her straight to the female pod. Since her charge was high profile, they had to be extra careful and place her around the right dangerous bitches. You didn't have too many women in Delaware getting booked for murder, and in order to be in the maximum security dorm, your ass better know how to braid, cook, or eat some pussy. If not, you must have been trained by Laila Ali her damn self, because the females surely weren't settling for less behind their concrete walls.

As the door for the main entrance opened, Faith stared at the doors that were aligned down the corridor. A few women sat around watching the small television mounted against the wall, and some sat in small groups, conversing at a low volume. It was like a bright movie theater, and Faith was the new film. She kept her head straight forward as the officer led her to the cell, which was door number seventeen, and opened it slowly.

"Hey Black Girl. You got a new cellie." The white woman tapped on the door with her police radio.

Watching the huge woman step out of the bed, Faith gasped. She stood around 6'2" tall. Her skin was dark milk chocolate and smooth. Her ass and hips carried the most weight on her perfectly-toned frame. Her eyes were dark brown, and her hair was braided neatly to the back in two individual plaits. Her pretty doll face resembled a woman with innocence, one who couldn't do any wrong, but the frown she was wearing at the moment caused the rookie officer to give Faith a farewell pat on the back before leaving her for dead.

"You gonna stand in my doorway or come the fuck in?"

"Yeah," Faith stuttered as she carried in the net bag full of clothes and hygiene products.

"What's your name?" Black Girl asked, moving over to the sink to wash her hands and face.

"Uhh, Faith. My name's Faith," she said twice, as if she wasn't sure.

"What are you locked up for?"

Faith tossed her property on the bed and exhaled. "I think I'm being framed for murder."

"You think?" Black Girl looked at her with a raised eyebrow. "You ain't one of them bitches who play with that meth is it?" Her voice was thick and serious.

"No, I don't do drugs. I mean, I think someone is setting me up. I didn't kill anyone."

Black girl smirked before shaking her head. "Look, I only got a few simple rules. Don't touch my shit. Shut the fuck up when I'm asleep. And don't allow anybody in my fucking room. If you break any one of those small obligations, I'll beat yo' fucking ass. Easy," she stated before grabbing her CD player from out of the locker box.

Faith wanted to bite the slick comment, but decided to be the bigger woman and jumped up on her top bunk. The torment of being in jail was already starting to kick in. It was hard to digest the situation when she thought about it. Not to mention, Faith didn't know that she was shacking in the room with one of the most dangerous women in Delaware. The aggravation was beyond the limit, and Wicked had placed the thought in her head to remind Ryan that he was gonna be a problem. All she needed to do was hear his voice. He wasn't picking up from the wall phone, and it was probably because of the hurt from dealing with Precious's death. Still and all, Ryan had to know that she wouldn't stoop that low to risk their child or her life because of a female who was giving him a little attention.

Lying back on the clear mattress, Faith waited patiently until they called her name for the attorney visit Markie D promised. It was the only hope she had left.

* * *

Two hours later
Ryan's spot, Northside, Philly, Cedar Street

"So you telling me that it ain't no other option? This man just pulls up and says that you work for him, and you gotta accept that shit?" Nas looked at Ryan awkwardly.

"Nigga, I ain't have no choice, and not only that, I feel like Lucci really feels like I has something to do with Precious being murdered. I ain't never had any press on me, period, but the nigga crept up on some real John Wick shit. It was like he didn't walk or move from how quiet this man crept up behind me," Ryan said as he passed the blunt around in a circle.

"That nigga probably a cop his damn self," Demerea chimed in.

"I was just about to say the same shit. How the fuck he talking about somebody else the police, but he want you to keep sliding in on these folks' meetings like you ain't spying for him or something?" Freddie walked around in the living room, evaluating the story, and had to put his opinion in.

"I wouldn't give a damn what he wanted me to do. I said the nigga offered me two million dollars. I'm just trying to make sure that all of us are safe in the process. I already accepted the deal, so it's really no other options."

"I mean, that is a lot of dough." Nas rubbed his chin. "That doesn't mean that this cat ain't got no slick shit going on either though. Plus you said that these people are dangerous also. It's a sticky situation, but I would approach it slowly. Nothing is more important than your safety, bro."

"He's right." Demerea nodded. "All this talking about fucking millions. You need half of that shit up front. How do we know this nigga ain't about to make you pull a dummy move and trick you? He ain't gotta give you shit, and he could be the same busta-ass nigga working with those same people to see if you're really solid or not."

"What type of person would buy thirty keys of dope just to see if I'm willing to trade on someone else? Trust me." Ryan stood up on his feet. "It's more to it than just that."

"Well whatever it is, you got us here, my guy. I ain't got nothing else better to do besides run up the bands, 'cause this shit ain't about to last for long," Nas agreed.

The knocking that erupted on his front door caused everyone to grow quiet. No one budged at first, so Demerea took the step to see who the hell was trying to be noticed so early in the afternoon. She gazed through the peephole before looking back at Ryan. She unlocked the latch and opened it, allowing DJ to step through the front entrance. His black Tommy Hilfiger hoodie hung over his head, and a pair of crisp Levi 504 slim fit jeans matched the Black Timberland boots on his feet. He took a seat on the opposite couch from Ryan. He looked around at everybody.

"Wassup? Why the hell y'all get so quiet when I walked in?"

Demerea didn't waste any time tooting her nose before walking to the back.

"What the fuck is her problem?" DJ shrugged, looking at Freddie, Ryan, and Nas.

Ryan stood up from his spot, grabbing the bridge of his nose. "So, me and you have been friends now forever. I thought it was supposed to be a mutual respect between us that we never crossed, DJ."

"Ryan, what the hell are you talking about?" He leaned forward.

"Nigga, you fucked Faith?"

The room grew extremely quiet, and DJ's face lowered in guilt. "Who told you that?

"What? Who told me? Why the fuck does that matter? Nigga, did you fuck her or not?" Ryan barked more aggressively.

"Bro, that shit was way before we met you."

Rushing over to DJ, Ryan tackled him down to the floor and landed a punch square on his jaw. "Fake-ass motherfucker! I trusted you.

Before he could hit him again, Freddie snatched them apart. DJ jumped up with his nostrils flaring like a bull.

"Nigga, you could have just shot a fade with me if you felt like sneaking me."

"Bitch nigga, I'll demolish you. I should have never trusted ya busta ass anyway. Always smiling in my bitch's face like you her brother and shit!"

"Nigga, I didn't tell you because it was before y'all met. I didn't want to ruin anything y'all had going on, Ryan. That was me trying to be a good friend, stupid."

"Nah, you got it backwards, idiot. If you were a real friend, you would've told me out of respect. Real friends ain't 'bout to smash each other's baby mamas and wait til the kid gets here to decide which one of them bitches is yours, DJ. You fake, nigga, and it ain't shit that's gonna change that." Ryan shoved Freddie's hands off him.

Taking a second to calm down, DJ circled around the sectional, where Nas cornered him. Even though he didn't have anything to do with the conversation they were speaking on, Nas refused to let two niggas he had mad love for fight like dogs on the fucking street.

"So you mean to tell me that you gonna let our friendship go down because of something that happened before you, Ryan? I accept how you feel about me not telling you, but I'm not about to sit here and let you call me a snake. I've had your back since we started rocking. Money moves and all. Nigga, we fam." DJ slammed a fist repeatedly against his chest.

"Man, nigga, shut the fuck up and get out my fucking spot! We ain't friends, and we ain't family. I'll never forgive you for no shit like this. The only regrets I have is getting that slut-ass bitch pregnant and thinking that you was my fucking homie. Now get the fuck out my shit!" Ryan spat.

"So that's how you really feel, my nigga?" DJ lowered his tone in shock from his friend's sharp words.

"You still here, nigga? Step!" Ryan pointed at the door.

Demerea stood against the hallway wall, looking on with a small smirk. She knew that DJ didn't want the secret to be revealed, but the shit could only be contained so long. It wasn't her business, but after the shit Faith pulled, she felt that Ryan deserved to know.

Grabbing his phone off the floor, DJ nodded. "Say less, my nigga. You ain't gotta worry about hearing from me again." He walked out of Ryan's apartment, slamming the door behind him.

Ryan looked back at Demerea and smirked. "Remember that slime-ass motherfuckers can't prosper with us. We can all eat, but where is the loyalty if niggas hide things from each other? That nigga knows all my movements, and ain't no telling where his mind at. I'm letting all y'all know right now. If his ass makes a false move, he's getting his ass killed. Simple. If it's gonna be us eating at the table, then so be it, but if you ain't gonna keep the loyalty first, you might as well walk out behind him." Ryan looked back and forth between them all.

Demerea was the first to take her seat back on the couch. "I'm just waiting to see what you need me to do next. You know where we stand," she confirmed.

Freddie and Nas looked at each other before taking seats back around the table.

"I guess we all on the same page." Ryan nodded and then heard his cell ring. He glanced down at the unfamiliar number. He stood up and headed into the kitchen.

Chapter 6

Walking in the small attorney room for her visit, Faith wiped the corners of her eyes. After a few hours of sleep, an officer alerted her to get ready, and that felt like one of the happiest moments of her life. After two minutes of sitting in the room alone, a tall white Jewish man stepped through the other side of the booth. A small white beanie that resembled a kufi was on the back of his head. His suit was big, but expensive, and his glasses had a black tint that covered his eyes completely. He kind of resembled the evil Mr. Smith from the movie *Matrix Reloaded.*

He pulled out his chair and took a seat. "Hello, Ms. Anderson. How are you holding up?"

"Not well, but I guess I don't have a choice," she replied before shaking his hand. "Are you the lawyer my father hired?"

"Kinda sorta. My name is Jeff Hovecek. Your dad paid me a small retainer fee to work on your case, but unfortunately, I would need the rest of the money in order to proceed. I started to dig in your file just because he made the effort, and I know how it feels to have a family sitting in a cell without the proper funds for representation. I began to scan through your case and what the state has against you, and it's not much, from what I see. They claim to have a video from the neighbor's camera across the street, and a few witnesses who heard you speaking irrationally the night before this girl was murdered. Now I would like to hear your side of the story, but as I said, I don't want to get too far into this without knowing how the payment will be handled." He crossed one leg over the other, sitting back in the small chair.

Faith exhaled, knowing that cash was the last thing she had at that moment. "How much does my father still owe?"

"Well, he gave me the retainer fee yesterday of eight grand, and he said it was all of his savings. I charged six just to look into it. If you would like me to proceed with the case, it will be an additional thirty-four thousand."

The large number nearly made her faint. Anything dealing with thousands in the double digits was surely out of the way. She knew that Ryan was the only one who had any chance to give up a number like that. The only question was if he would help or not. "The only person I know that might help is my child's father, but the victim was his friend, so I haven't really talked to him since all of this happened. I need a call," Faith explained.

Jeff Hovecek exhaled with an iffy grin. "I'm not really allowed to make phone calls to any victims, or relatives of the victims, but if it's your child's father, I can make an exception. But only if it's about the retainer fee." He pulled out a nice cell phone and looked up at her. "Do you have a number for him?" Listening to the digits she was calling out, he entered them on his dial pad and pressed the send button. He placed it on speaker. Faith silently prayed that he would answer once the line began to ring lightly. On the fifth ring, when her lawyer was about to hang up, Ryan's voice came through the phone.

"Who is this?"

Jeff Hovecek placed the phone towards Faith so she could speak. "Ryan? It's me," she replied in a sad tone.

"Faith! What the fuck are you calling my phone for? You got a lot of nerve after what you did, bitch."

"Ryan, please listen. I didn't hurt Precious. I never would do something like that, no matter what we were going through. You know that I'm not that type of person, Ryan. Just think about it." Faith was trying to talk some sense into his head.

"Who did it then, Faith? You were the only one mad. You were the only one shooting threats in the air towards this girl, all because I said that I didn't want to be with you. I told you that shit was gonna be good, and you didn't listen. You made it this way, and you need to stand up for your actions. In the end, it doesn't matter what I believe, Faith. It's those people you have to prove it to. I don't want any parts of that, and I'm still not in the clear with this girl's family. What else is there to talk about?"

"My lawyer, Ryan. I need help paying him to prove my innocence. Now I can pay you back once I come home and get a job, but don't let these people take me away from Prince like this. You're the only one who can help me," she stressed. His voice went silent for a second until she called his name. "Ryan?"

"Faith, your mom is part of the reason you're sitting in there right now. No one is standing beside you - not even family. This isn't a joke, and by the time you understand that, it'll be too fucking late. Maybe you need to ask her for help, because I don't have none for you. Precious really meant something to me, and now you have to face this shit on your own. Please don't call my phone anymore," he said before hanging up the line.

Faith was at a loss for words. Her mind was so distraught from the call that she didn't even know what to say. Jeff Hovecek shook his head, and placed the phone back into his pocket. "I'm sorry, Ms. Anderson. Maybe me and your father can try and go through some steps to getting the payment another way. I have a few people who can look into your case for a cheaper price also," he offered.

Faith mustered a fake smile before shaking his hand. "Sure. If anything is possible, that would be a great help from you."

"I'll be in contact. Just keep your head up and give it a little time. You may have to sit for a while, but it's better to allow things to accumulate for you."

Standing up from her chair, Faith nodded and left the attorney booth without another word.

The statement from Ryan's mouth nearly had her in tears. The thought of him actually feeling that she did murder Precious was ridiculous. It was obvious he was in love with Precious, but it still gave him no right to doubt the word of the woman who had given birth to his child.

Making her way back to the dormitory, all Faith could think about was the night of the party. Her head was discombobulated the morning after the party to the point where she couldn't remember a thing. It was all a blur, but she damn well knew that she didn't murder that bitch.

After entering the pod, she made her way inside the room and looked at herself in the mirror. She didn't want to stress herself about the situation, but reality was really kicking in that she might be sitting for a while.

Black Girl raised her head, and sat up straight in the bed. "So how did your attorney visit go?" She was staring at Faith's little backside like a fat kid looked at a Little Debbie cake.

"Not good. Don't really wanna talk about it." Faith continued to bend over as she looked in the mirror, wiping the corners of her eyes.

Black Girl licked her lips and shook her head. "I understand. It happens to a lot of girls who come in this dorm. If you don't mind me asking, have you ever been with a girl before? You have a nice-ass body for a little chick."

The remark sent anger flowing through Faith's body like a heat missile. The time for her smart, nasty-ass comments was definitely not about to be dismissed, and in order to get some understanding, she was about to check that shit before the bitch could continue to get out of hand. Turning around from the mirror to face Black Girl, Faith placed a hand on her hip.

"Look, bitch. I don't know who the fuck you think I am, but I'm not about to be playing around with you in this motherfucker. I'm not gay, and I'm damn sho' not feeling no big giant-ass hoe like you. I got a lot going on, and before you keep getting besides yourself like you some type of chain gang Debo, we gonna end that shit right now. Watch your fucking mouth and leave me alone!" Faith spat.

Black Girl laughed before waving her off. "Bitch, I just asked you a question. I know you just came back from the little attorney visit and you mad, so I'll let that slide, but you can calm down with all that fake-ass gangsta murda mama shit cause I'll beat yo' ass a new hairdo in this bitch."

"Nah, fuck that." Faith folded her arms. "You ain't gonna do shit to me, and if you think that I'm sweet just because I'm little, yo' ass gonna have a rude awakening in this cell. You need to tread carefully and leave me alone, because I don't take threats lightly. "

Black Girl set her CD player down on the bed and wiggled the edge of her ear. "What the fuck you just say, hoe?"

Faith could already tell where the small argument was leading, so she decided to be the reason it went all the way. The stories of bitches getting beaten to death in prison were damn sure not about to have her name on the same list. "Let me repeat myself so you can hear a little better!" Faith yelled before hauling off and punching Black Girl in the side of her head. She followed up with a two-piece to her face.

The next punch was caught easily by Black Girl's hand. The moment Faith witnessed the big bitch stand to her feet, she gasped. Black Girl landed a hard fist directly on Faith's eye, nearly knocking her unconscious. By the time she hit the floor, she was gasping for air and trying to shake the dizziness that was rattling her brain. She didn't expect the foot that came next, crashing hard into her stomach, forcing her to roll over in pain.

"I'm sorryyyy!" was all she could let out before Black Girl grabbed her by the hair forcefully.

"Now since you wanna play tough, bitch, I'ma just take that shit. I told you to watch yo' mouth. Now you gonna get yo' ass up, pull them pants down, and fold yo' li'l slim goodie ass up on that bed. I'ma give you fifteen seconds, and if you can't get it right, I'ma knock you the fuck out again. Do you understand what the fuck I'm saying?" Black Girl whispered lightly into her ear.

"Y-yes!" Faith groaned in pain.

Releasing Faith's hair, Black Girl backed up, allowing her to stand. Faith trembled in fear as she tried to stand. Her legs were looser than a ten year old bike chain and her head was thumping with tremendous pain as she watched the huge woman tower over her.

"Hurry up! Pull them britches off and fold yo' ass up, now!"

Faith did as she was told and removed her pants and panties.

"Now lay back on my fucking bed. You make any false move, I'ma cut yo' fucking throat," Black Girl threatened through clenched teeth.

Lying back on the bed, Faith dropped a small tear, knowing that it was possibly her last day on earth. Watching Black Girl drop her pants, Faith's heart sped up tremendously.

Pushing Faith's little legs back to her shoulders, Black Girl mugged her. "Since you wanna be hard, you my bitch now, hoe. Do you understand?"

Faith nodded her head at a fast pace, and her chest was heaving harder than a muthafucka.

Black girl didn't waste any time wrapping her lips around Faith's sweet spot, sucking and licking at a fast pace. Faith closed her eyes in fear, wishing that she could be saved from the torment. Her tense body soon began to relax after the first minute. She tried to think about something other than what was going on at the moment, but for some reason, she couldn't. The small tingles and feelings from Black Girl's tongue were starting to be felt more by the second, so she tried to envision Ryan making love to her. The saddest thing passed her mind, and she had to admit that Ryan couldn't even make her feel the way this bitch was as she was digging her tongue inside her kitty. After accepting the fact that she was being raped by a big pretty bitch, a slight moan escaped her lips. Black Girl paused after hearing her and smiled.

Faith opened her eyes and looked down at her nervously. "Keep going," she whispered.

"Of course," Black Girl replied before burying her head back down into her sweet spot.

Chris Green

Chapter 7
DJ's spot, Severe and Teona

After sitting across from DJ's spot for hours, Severe began to grow agitated. The mission was quite simple. Detective Bradley wanted Ryan's ass dead in a certain amount of time, and if the mission wasn't handled, that led all the bullshit back to him. Teona's nasty ass had been running around with him for the past two days filling his head up with knowing the whereabouts of this nigga, but no one had seen a sign of him yet.

After taking a swig of the Brisk iced tea, Teona threw the can out of his car window and burped loudly. Severe looked at her with a dirty frown.

"Bitch, say excuse me! You been getting mighty comfortable, Teona. I said that I was willing to pay you for telling me where Ryan rests his head, and we ain't had no luck yet. Wassup with that?"

"Nigga, we gotta just have patience. Ever since that nigga killed my sisters, he been laying low 'cause he know everybody gonna be on his ass. Don't just act like this is only about me either, 'cause I'm doing you a favor too!" she spat back.

"Bitch, what favor? The only reason I even know you is because of Tyleema and Sekoya, and them bitches been robbing since they were sixteen. It's bound to happen to yo' ass when you playing in the streets. So for that I'm sorry, but right now, this ain't about them. I'm trying to handle the business that we agreed on. You said Ryan would be at this fucking spot, and we ain't seen him yet."

"And just like I said, you gotta have patience, motherfucker." Teona pointed, spotting the black '96 Impala pulling up in front of the home.

Severe grabbed the handle of his pistol. He waited until the driver's side door came open, but paused when he saw DJ exit the vehicle. "Is that him?" He looked over at Teona.

"No, that's his friend DJ, but I told you this is where they duck off at. If he's still migrating back and forth over here, that means Ryan is somewhere lurking in the cut also. You just gotta wait. If you touch him, Ryan isn't gonna show. These niggas already be on some high alert shit anyway."

Severe eased his hand off the chrome 9mm handgun and stared at DJ. The time for Ryan's ass was slowly ticking down, and he wasn't about to miss the opportunity to be a part of the table. If it meant holding off a little longer, that's what it was gonna be.

* * *

After pulling up in front of his home, DJ hopped out of his whip and headed up the driveway. The incident with Ryan had him on edge because that small secret with Faith was never supposed to get out. It was a mistake that occurred when they were younger, and out of respect for his boy, he didn't want to seem like a hater by telling him given the strong relationship that they were starting to build over the years. Nothing was more important than friendship, and he honestly felt that he was doing the right thing, but shit turned sour faster than he could imagine. Ryan's birthday was right around the corner, and the recent shit he had planned for him was now about to go out the window, because Ryan damn sure made it clear that their friendship was totally over.

His phone buzzing stopped him in his tracks. He was hoping that maybe it was Ryan wanting to talk the shit out. DJ stared at the long bill collecting-looking number. He decided to answer. The operator for the Delaware detention center began to speak in his ear, causing him to listen carefully. Once he heard Wicked's name, his heart skipped a beat. Pressing five, he listened as the call connected and spoke through the line. "Yo, bro?"

"Wassup, nigga? Long time, no hear. You must ain't got love for a nigga no mo'?" Wicked asked with a slight hint of hostility in his voice.

"What?" DJ glanced at the phone like he was talking to the cops. "Nigga, I ain't heard from you since them folks had the sentencing hearing. You just fell off the face of the earth, Wicked. Of course we got love for you. We family, fool."

"I can't tell, if you still running around with Ryan."

"Wicked, what are you talking about? Ryan is the same nigga I been moving with. Why the hell would that change?" DJ sensed the bullshit through his small statements.

"You know why. That nigga got my fucking cousin whacked, and ain't nobody did nothing about it," he whispered through the line.

"What? Wicked, I don't know what the hell you been smoking in there, but you definitely got the wrong information. Reckless was killed in front of a police station by some gangbanging-ass niggas. Some shit that he got in the mix of without thinking. Why the hell would Ryan have any reason to do that? And he's not even stupid enough to pull no shit like that. Your cousin was out here wigging, nigga. He was taking niggas' shit. Popping people left and right. I hate to say it, li'l bro, but he brought his fate on himself. Plus you need to remember that you on a recorded phone call. Watch the way you speaking, bro. Please," DJ warned, feeling that Wicked had just insulted his best friend.

"That's a fucking lie and you know it. See you too, scary DJ. You've been a do-boy for that fuck nigga since middle school, and you always will be. It was known in the streets about that small-ass beef between Reckless and him, and just because I been gone don't mean that I can't find out what the fuck is shaking, dummy. My fucking cousin is gone, and word is coming from more than one mouth. Free is spitting Ryan's name for the number one contender, and what reason do he got to lie if he the one who handled the business, DJ? See, one thing I learned, no matter how hard you try to hide shit, it has a way of coming to the light. I happened to be sliding through medical today and ran across Faith. Seems like she stressing the same issue. Her dirty dog-ass baby daddy is the one who calling the shots out there handling all that business," Wicked spat.

Shaking his head, DJ chuckled. "Bro, you really losing it, because I know Faith ain't told you no shit like that. It's a lie, idiot. You got yo' head wrapped in ya ass because your family gone, but he killed himself, Wicked. No one else did shit. Stop stressing, bro, stop saying that shit, because it's not true. Now I don't know what's up with you, and I know you mad, but if you gonna be hitting me up on some shit like this, lose my number. I can send you money or whatever to make sure you good, but I'm not 'bout to let you just spazz out and keep spitting crazy shit through my line, nigga. If you felt this way, you could've just called Ryan your damn self."

DJ looked back at the car that was slowly pulling off from across the street. He thought that his eyes were playing tricks on him, but it kinda looked like Teona sitting in the passenger seat with a nigga who looked pretty familiar. Feeling that his mind was just moving in overload, DJ focused back on the stupid phone call that was at hand.

Wicked laughed through the line before growing quiet for a slight second. "I'ma just say this and be done with it. I come home soon. I'm killing you, and him, and anybody else who I felt like had a part of that shit, nigga. That's word on my mama. I don't give a fuck about no police, no Ryan, or none of that fake-ass King of Delaware shit. This is what y'all fuck boys wanted to cook up. Now I'ma show you what that real Arizona heat is about, nigga. Mark that shit in yo' fuck-ass head," Wicked threatened.

"See you when you get home, nigga." DJ hung up the phone, not wanting to reply back over the hot-ass jail phone. Wicked was truly talking greasy if he really felt like they had something to do with Reckless getting murdered. From the sound of his voice, DJ knew that shit was surely gonna get out of hand, but the information he spilled was even more critical. Ryan was in his feelings at the wrong time, and shit was sounding shaky, especially when Faith's name was in the pot of bad news.

There was officially some slime shit taking place, and Ryan was the one about to fall directly in the center.

Chris Green

Chapter 8
Two days later
The Midnight Cartel meeting
11:43 p.m.

Ryan whipped his Infiniti truck inside the parking lot of the small country-ass bar. Ryan stepped out, feeling the sharp wind that was cutting hard as hell. A few cars passed by the lot, and the streets were nearly deserted from one end to the next. It felt so awkward, and the thought of Ghost's words pumped through his mind as he stood by the side of his truck and sparked a small joint. His hands were slightly trembling from the thought of Richard playing a hardcore trick on him. What if this nigga Ghost really was a decoy for him to see if trading was on his mind? Shit was so jumbled in his brain, but the time for turning around was over. The meeting was a few minutes away from being started, and before he went out bad, he would die a soldier in that muthafucka.

After checking the clip of his gun, he tucked it tightly on his hip, grabbed the large bag of money, and headed for the entrance. A black Polo skull cap was pulled down over his eyes, giving him enough vision to see whatever he needed to, and the large leather jacket he wore concealed the handle of his weapon perfectly. When he walked up to the two bodyguards, they allowed him to enter. Ryan nodded and continued inside.

Unlike most nights, the small bar was packed to the fullest capacity. People moved around the floor, passing around drinks and vibing to that old raggedy-ass jukebox that sat in the corner. Most of the faces in the building were white, of course. The few black people that bounced around that bitch were looking clueless, and that's when

Ryan really started to piece shit together. Half of the citizens in the room were definitely decoys. No one was really sipping the beverages being tossed, and the most you could see was a little nicotine smoke flying in the air. Instead of panicking, he decided to stay focused, and he moved towards the counter. Once Lizzy's eyes landed on him, she flashed Ryan the biggest smile ever.

"Hey, papa catfish. I'm glad you was able to get through without a hassle. Go ahead on down." She pointed to the secret basement door with a wink.

"Thanks, Liz," Ryan spoke over the loud country music. He headed off to his destination.

Ryan stepped through the door, closed it gently behind him, and walked slowly down the flight of steps. After getting to the bottom, a horrible stench attacked his nostrils. It was like that nasty pussy smell when a junkie wanted to let you hit it for a crack rock or some shit. Covering his nose, Ryan held the bag of money, walked up to the steel door, and knocked three times. He glanced at his watch. It was 11:53; seven minutes to spare. It didn't take long before the metal peephole latch slid openly roughly. Once the bodyguard recognized Ryan, he closed it and opened the door for him to enter.

"They're waiting for you," he said aggressively, like he hadn't gotten any breakfast before his wife started her daily slut routines. It was always a different attitude with buddy every time Ryan stepped foot into the meeting room, but of course, it was normal for a man who was only allowed so much attention.

Richard's face brightened once Ryan stepped around the corner. The ten other table members were already seated and Detective Bradley, who hadn't been seen in a while, was posted against the door of that creepy-ass office. His face was tight, like he wasn't too happy to see Ryan walk through that bitch with his quota.

Placing the bag on the floor in front of Richard, Ryan shook his hand. "Good to see you, Richard. Hopefully I'm not too late."

"Oh no, you're just in time, Ryan. Please take your seat," he replied.

Summer walked over to receive the duffle bag, and she walked it back through the small office room, closing the door behind her. The silence crowded the room, and the only noise that could be heard was the small gathering above their heads. Richard paced around in small circles, glancing at his watch every other second until the time finally came. Once the two hands of the clock landed on twelve, he clasped his hands together.

"Good evening, everyone. Welcome to the meeting. I've been alerted to some disturbing news in the past few days - and I mean real disturbing news. You know, it's like a kid who can't learn to stop shitting in their diaper. They'll keep doing it until you show them how to use the toilet, but in this case, we have grown individuals who keep spilling the same stinky clumps of shit in their overgrown fucking pants," he mouthed slowly, stressing his anger.

Ryan instantly began to grow nervous from the statement. Shit was already too intense with the recent episode at Lucci Bruno's spot, and it was obvious that every time Richard gave the stupid speech of someone fucking up, their brains ended up spilling on the muthafucka sitting next to them. Ryan didn't waste any time clutching his gun handle just in case shit looked sour.

The sight of Summer walking back out of the room to join her twin told him that some shit was definitely finna get to cracking in that bitch. Everyone remained silent as Richard started to speak again.

"Now I've done my investigation, and the results have come back conclusive. It seems like we have a few slackers at this table. And when I say a few, I mean a lot. What do you think about that, Ryan?" He looked over to him with an evil-ass smile.

The bubbles in Ryan's stomach were tightening, and he truly wanted to pull his gun and start shooting at whoever he could in order to get up out of there. Exhaling calmly, he answered, "Slackers are bad. I mean, you can't possibly get anywhere with those. To be honest, Richard, I kinda wanted this to be my last drop because my folks are out there putting all the work on me, and I don't have enough time to handle enough shit on my end."

Richard's expression grew angry. "I'm afraid that just can't happen that way, Ryan. See, the reason I'm asking you is because you, along with three other people, have been the only ones meeting the quota for the table. See, you are like the Michael Jordan of this group, Ryan. Your vicious talent has come into the picture and taken the show. I'm the vicious coach on the side who's willing to slit a few throats in order to make sure the team shines," he replied while sliding off his suit jacket. "Do you understand what I mean, Ryan?

"Not really. You kind of lost me after you started talking about basketball," he replied truthfully.

The rest of the table sat in silence as Richard looked around to see if any of them had anything to say. The one woman who usually added a thousand opinions was quiet as a mouse. Simion from Georgia was sitting back like he owned the fucking world, and judging from his expression, he wasn't placed in the category with all the slackers. Richard was trying to explain a message without everyone understanding, but he was damn sure about to make it clear enough.

"Everyone, Ryan, has grown confused as to what I'm speaking about, and that makes me feel bad. We are all a family. A team. Since we've built this team, the same shit has occurred, even when it was just one motherfucker sitting at this table with me. Winter, can I have your pistol please?" Richard asked politely.

Watching the woman pass Richard a chrome .45 Kimber automatic, Ryan's body tensed.

"I'm very disappointed in the actions of my table. I explained this to you all numerous times that if the boss lady is mad, then I'm also furious. Not to mention Ryan still doesn't understand I'm saying. So I wanna make this clear for him."

Richard placed a slug through the head of the man sitting on the far right end of the table. He followed with the man directly next to him, and did the same thing until he reached Ryan's chair. By the time he was done, six people laid dead in their chairs, and the room was sitting in shock. Ryan's gun was now out under the table, but his fingers felt like glue. The horrible scene caused him to shake horribly, and that's when he knew shit was deeper than a hooker's cooch. Six people's heads were nearly blown away from their shoulders, and he couldn't help but to look at their bodies dangling out of the chairs.

"What the fuck?" Ryan mumbled with his teeth jittering loudly.

Simion from Atlanta looked over to Ryan and yawned. His posture was too fucking cool, and it was obvious this shit was planned. After killing six members of the table, four men remained: Ryan, Simion, and the two others that were from out of state.

Richard huffed before chuckling loudly. He gave Winter back her weapon. She looked over at Ryan and forced a sly smile. They were on some next level shit in the basement meetings, and that now explained why there were so many people upstairs: to block out the sound of what was about to occur.

Sitting back at the table, Richard looked over to Ryan, and spoke. "That's what I mean, Ryan. These people have failed to deliver their end of the bargain, and unfortunately, that can't be tolerated. You, on the other hand, have accumulated more profits than those six people together. This is the reason you can't just quit. You are the key, Ryan. We never needed these assholes. Look at them." Richard laughed, pointing towards the dead bodies like a maniac. "They disobeyed and reaped the consequences. Ryan, you're a good man, but I don't wanna shoot you in the fucking head. You're the best worker I've seen in a long time. Not too many have your capabilities of flipping forty kilos of cocaine in a week. That's the reason we eliminated the problem. You along with Simion, Preston, and Sage are the reason why we are prospering weekly with this movement. Because we all know if the money stops, the table stops, and that means I have to hear the boss lady's anger."

The words "boss lady" continued to run through Ryan's ears and that reinforced the things that Ghost was spitting to him a few days before. Richard was definitely not in charge of the shit that was at hand. Provoking his anger was something that Ryan didn't want to do, so telling him that he was about to quit selling dope was now out of the question. "I understand."

Richard jumped to his feet as if he had caught the Holy Ghost. "He understands, you guys. We are all back on track, baby. Summer, Winter, could you dolls handle this little mess that we have in the room? I think it's about time for us to get a smaller table."

The girls nodded in silence and started to drag the dead bodies out of the chairs one by one. These bitches were moving around like it was the movie *Hostel*. The weirdest shit was that these bitches had the nerve to drag these niggas' bodies inside that same creepy-ass small office. There was no telling what the hell was going on in that room, because you damn sho' couldn't see anything when it was time for the door to come open.

Richard walked over and took the seat next to Ryan. "Listen, kid. You've been a very valuable asset to what I have placed in effect here. The money is lovely, and I guarantee I'll make you rich within the next few months if you just listen. You don't deserve what these assholes got here tonight, Ryan. You're a star pupil." He held up his hands like that shit was gonna comfort a nigga.

"How do I know I won't end up like them?" Ryan said nervously with his eyes trying to study the man in front of him.

Richard leaned forward with a crooked smile. "You're fine, Ryan. Just don't leave, son. You could make a great addition to this group if we follow the rules and move in silence. Do your job, and I'll make you untouchable. I don't see you making me mad, Ryan, and that's a good sign. Lizzy will be waiting for you upstairs. In three months, you should be sitting at the head of these seats, my friend. Maybe we can even be business partners together." Richard held out his hand with a wry smile.

Ryan knew that accepting his gesture would surely mean a bundle of bullshit. But regardless of his personal feelings, he knew that rejecting his offer wouldn't end too well. Instead of going with his first mind, he shook Richard's hand sternly. "Hopefully you can keep your word on that, man."

"My words are only broken if you feel otherwise, Ryan. I don't see otherwise coming into the bounds of our relationship." Richard patted him on the shoulder and got back up to his feet. Glancing down at his watch, he smiled. "Well, it's that time, people. Meeting adjourned. Be sure to remember that things have slimmed down to a narrow few. It's only us, which means that you can't trust nobody, not even yourselves. That concludes the meet-up for this week, and you guys can check in with Lizzy before you exit the building." Richard dismissed them and headed through the small office door.

Rushing to get the hell out of there, Ryan made his way back upstairs. The sight of six motherfuckers dying at once wasn't something easily stomached. The devil's idea was to keep moving the work and become rich, and Ryan wasn't debating with money or death. The drug game was over with him for good. If Richard wanted his drugs sold, Ghost was gonna be the new clientele for his ass.

Climbing up the stairs of terror, Ryan high-stepped to the counter. He nearly rushed into a customer trying to get Lizzy's attention.

"Hey honey, your little trash route is out by the car. Somebody already did your first stop. You're all set." She walked past him and quickly pushed on to please the group of guests.

Not understanding her fully, he listened to the instructions and headed back for his truck. Stepping outside, he passed the two bodyguards and moved towards his truck. The sight of Detective Bradley posted on his side door made it clear that some bullshit was in the air.

"Mr. Royal. I haven't seen you in a while, my guy. You must have forgotten about our agreements on those payments?"

"Nigga, I don't owe you shit. I been slaving nearly two months getting off these folks' shit and you ain't did nothing. Why the hell I gotta keep paying you for?"

Bradley leaned off his vehicle with the garbage bag full of kilos. "'Cause I'm the reason you're still living. You must not see how this works, Royal. It don't matter what you sell or how many you move. It only takes the wrong shit to pull, and you're dead. I heard about your little incident out in Philly. You think just because you travel thirty minutes away from Wilmington that we won't hear about you being mixed up in the murder of a college graduate?"

"It doesn't matter what you heard. I ain't do shit. Now what you can do is give me my damn supply and let me push on about my business, Bradley. Me and you don't have nothing to speak on - unless you wanna go back in there and explain to Richard why I can't complete the job he asked me to do?" Ryan pointed a finger to the bar's entrance.

Dropping the large bag of cocaine on the ground, Detective Bradley stepped over to him until they stood face to face. "I'm gonna let you know something, Royal. I don't know why you feel like I'm just the old regular officer who's not in the loop of every dirty muthafucka around this bitch. I'm the one who brought you into this game. Now I don't know if you think this shit is a game, but I can promise you, without me, you'll be dead after four more runs. I don't give a damn if you can push two hundred keys in a week, little boy," he threatened in anger.

Ryan quickly scooped up the heavy bag and tossed it in his back seat. "That's the thing about me, Bradley. I don't give a damn what you think. Right now, this business is between me and Richard. You're only a middle man that's holding my fucking nuts to get some paper. Those days are over. If I'm selling weight for the table, there is no extortion. I'm not paying shit." Ryan mugged Richard before jumping in the driver's seat of his truck.

Ryan cranked the engine and rolled down his window before pulling off. "And just for the record, Richard chose me to have this position. That's your boss, right? Try putting in a complaint form and take up any form of grievance through the state, sucka-ass muthafucka!" Ryan spat before mashing the gas out of the parking lot.

Detective Bradley smiled while nodding his head at Ryan's car. Pulling out his phone, he dialed a set of numbers and placed it up to his ear. The call didn't ring more than two times before Severe picked up.

"Yeah?"

"I asked you to take care of the business, and you've failed. I'm not understanding how being a part of this table is your mission if you can't take care of something simple like getting rid of somebody. Is it me, or is it just that you're an idiot?" He looked around at the other members of the table, who were retreating to their cars.

"I tried, man. I've been moving around with this bitch for four days and all she's been doing is telling me to have patience. I just located where their little hangout is. All you have to do is give me a little more fucking time. I just can't jump out there and miss, muthafucka!" Severe yelled through the line.

"I think you need to watch your mouth, you punk, jelly bean-ass fuckboy. I'm the reason yo' bitch ass ain't serving a forty-eight year bid. I pushed for your charges to be dropped. If you have any form of common sense, and you wanna keep that pathetic-ass life of yours, I suggest you finish this agreement. Are we clear on that, my nigga?" Detective Bradley said with a nasty tone.

"Yeah, whatever, Bradley. Just have a little patience, man. I'm not risking myself just because you need to save your ass!" Severe spat before hanging up.

Detective Bradley smirked before sliding the phone back into his pocket. The insult from Ryan was one that wasn't going to be taken lightly. He had crossed boundaries that shouldn't have been broken, and now the gloves were coming off. When it came down to Bradley's money, he didn't give a damn whether you died or stayed alive. A face couldn't be present at that table if you were dead. Ryan was gonna be the first to see that shit didn't work on his time. Mr. Good Cop was officially over.

Chris Green

Chapter 9
Two days later
Precious's funeral
German Town funeral home.
8:30 a.m.

The ceremony for Precious was packed to capacity. Hundreds of people from her college were attending and mourning the death of their honor student. The award of the century was stamping her name and awarding a funding campaign to pay for her burial.

Ryan spoke on behalf of himself and the small friends she did meet during the time they had known each other. The horrific feeling was unreal, and definitely some of the best experiences in his life had been around Precious. His donation to her mother and father was Club Royal. Within months, she had built something that was worth a small price into a big empire. The club had been gaining popularity on behalf of the sweet, charming smile of Precious Edmond. It was a day that Ryan would never forget. Out of respect for her family, he signed the rights over to her parents as a gift so that his friend's legacy could continue on.

After Ryan was finished, a few more guests spoke on behalf of her school and the impact she made on students and teachers. The tears were running down numerous faces, and the pain in Ryan's heart was unbearable. He never thought that Faith would stoop so low as to kill someone because he didn't adore her anymore. Even more deceitful things came out once she was taken to County for the murder, shit that she could never apologize for. It could never be forgotten. Precious was a true piece of many people's lives and Faith was the reason she had been removed.

The burial was right after, and Ryan was quickly approached by Lucci Bruno. His eyes were puffy red, and the look on his Italian face was meaner than that of Al Capone himself.

"Ryan. I need to see you tomorrow. My spot. It's crazy that my niece is gone, and I just wanna hear the story to know exactly what took place. Please, if it's possible, kid. Be there." He gave Ryan a look that said it wasn't a debate.

"Sure, Lucci. I'll be there," Ryan agreed out of respect. The gut feeling in his stomach said that Lucci wanted to do more than ask a few questions.

Right after Lucci disappeared into the crowd, Mr. and Mrs. Edmond could be seen standing at the line where everyone shook their hands for sending great love for their daughter. His heart thumped harder with every second as he pushed closer. Once his face connected with her mom's, he instantly dropped a large face full of tears in regret. After all the catastrophe, his heart wasn't strong enough to admit the truth. Mrs. Edmond's expression slightly softened when she witnessed his tears. Wrapping her arms around Ryan, she embraced him into a hug.

"I'm sorry that this his happened to you, Mrs. Edmond. I love Precious with all of my heart. She will be a part of me forever."

Mrs. Edmond rubbed his shoulder. "We love our baby, and God called her home. It's nothing that you can blame yourself for. My daughter loved you for some reason, so that ties you with my family. We will always help you and be grateful for what you've done for my princess. "

"Thank you, Ms. Edmond. Please be sure to remain in touch for signing the papers for the club and for your friendship. You will always be my family indeed." Ryan looked at Mr. Edmond and shook his hand. "If there is anything that I can do for you, sir, please don't hesitate to ask."

"May God bless you, son. Just continue to strive and live for yourself. Remember that Precious is dear to us all, and that will remain a bond that we share. We appreciate that forever." He nodded his head with respect.

Before Ryan could walk off, Mrs. Edmond grabbed his wrist. "Please know that my brother Lucci is highly upset about this incident, and he's really not so good on letting things ease. Please be sure to stay away from him. Any offer should be denied from him," she mumbled lightly.

Taking that message to the brain, Ryan thanked her once more before continuing through the cemetery line.

It took over fifteen minutes to get back to his car after the sad moments of Precious's last gathering, but it wasn't gonna be in vain. She was gonna be remembered, because the game was finally about to be over with for him. All he had to do was play his cards and be sure to dodge his enemies.

Pulling off in his Infiniti truck. He was sure of one thing. There was no such thing as losing that battle.

* * *

Women's maximum security pod
11:33 a.m.

"So you mean to tell me that this nigga left you for another bitch, and this is the same girl that ended up dead?" Black Girl looked at Faith with a sad expression.

"Yes, girl. That's why it's so hard for me to believe. I mean, the bitch was lame for sneaking on the family I was building, but I wasn't trying to get that bitch."

They were on the fourth round of Casino with the playing cards, and Faith nearly had Black Girl in tears after explaining the entire story about what was occurring in her personal life.

"Listen. I know it might not be much, but I have a few dollars put up that I can help with if you would like. My mom owns a bonding company also. That's why I've been able to help out so many other chicks in here. The law work is kinda easy for me too. Trust me, before my mom had the connections she got, I had to push my own law work, but I still ended up being found guilty," Black Girl admitted.

Moving the hair from over her black eye, Faith took a bite out of the bag of chips from the lunch tray. After Faith spent a few days of being caged in with the 6'2" lesbian, Black Girl actually began to turn into the sweetest person ever. After her episode, she eventually showered Faith with food, other hygiene products, and rules on what not to do within the institution. It was weird to see her be stingy with letting certain people in the dorm kick it around Faith, but her reasons were good ones if she didn't like you. Everybody in the dorm loved Black Girl. She was a thorough bitch that kept shit in order when hoes wanted to get out of line in that four wall ring. Faith started to learn little rules from Black Girl that she didn't like, but she complied because mostly everything out of her mouth was real. But what kind of made Black Girl grow on her even more was the hurtful story of how she ended up in prison.

It seemed like she had the sunshine life when it came to relationships. She attended one of the best colleges up north, and she was also the star basketball player of the school. After high school, her lover Kenneth was granted the chance to be drafted to the NBA. He married Black Girl, and of course spoiled her to every measure, and she did the same in return. Within those two years, they got married. Two weeks after that, she came home to him cheating and blew his head off with his own pistol. Unfortunately, Miss Little Creep got the same. Black Girl overloaded and placed seven slugs in the woman's back. It was hurtful to see the young basketball star die months before his initiation into the NBA, but the passion of a broken-hearted woman was brought out of Black Girl when she caught another bitch riding on top of him in their bedroom.

Black Girl received two life sentences for the overkill on the two victims, and she had been back and forth to prison and the county fighting for her freedom. Her mom and her lawyer were shooting for a crime of passion since she was only eighteen when it happened, and now she was thirty-four. After sixteen years of incarceration, she accepted the fact that it would be a while before the people decided to let her ass go anywhere. Instead of crashing out and committing suicide like Black Girl planned, she began to take that pressure away with working out and hitting the books. Accomplishing major requirements behind the wall, she aced every college course she placed her hands into.

"Thanks, girl, but how can I accept any help from you when there's barely anyone doing what they're supposed to do for you? I can't believe you been locked up sixteen years."

Placing the cards down on the bed, Black Girl took a deep breath. "Look, this shit is only a mental thing. Most people come into prison and jail expecting to do the time, but eventually the time does them. It's hard some days, but you just gotta remember that it's in your mind. The people wanna keep you institutionalized for the sake of their pennies. That don't mean that I'ma let they ass make me a product. Since I've been doing time, I've learned two things. Anyone can turn on you, and never give the police the satisfaction of winning. "

"What do you mean?" Faith listened as if she was in elementary school again.

"It means exactly what I said. I'm for the inmates, not the police. I've gotten numerous assaults for slapping bitches out for letting that badge pump their head up. Ever since I've used my anger to get into those law books, I've been a beast. You gotta stay focused and just keep holding on to what's important."

"And what's that?" Faith shrugged her shoulders as if nothing was going to help a situation like prison.

Black Girl looked at her with a crooked smile. "Revenge."

Chapter 10

After arriving back home from Precious's funeral, Ryan sat around with Torey, Freddie, Nas, and Demerea. No one really spoke too much since Ryan was still grieving heavily over the loss of his friend.

Demerea moved around the house fixing the fellas drinks and lighting blunts back to back in order to kill the dull atmosphere. Whenever there were too many depressed niggas around, people had the tendency to die, and she didn't need any of these assholes acting up in the house due to a bad aura around that bitch.

"So if I can get this right, you expect us to keep trapping this work, and you telling me these people are really supposed to be the cops, nigga? What type of fucking plan you working up there in yo' fucking head, Ryan?" Torey asked with a straight face.

"It's no plan. It's just instincts, cuz. These people are forcing my hands, and ain't shit I can do about it. As long as I'm dealing with them alone, y'all don't have to worry about anything. I'm gonna take care of you or whatever you guys' cut is and continue to pull the necessary strings in order to end this shit. The dope game is over for me," Ryan clarified.

"So who is this other dude you were telling me about, this Ghost nigga? What does he have to do with this?" Nas was trying to really break down what the fuck was going on.

"Ghost is this motherfucker who obviously got a vendetta with these cops or whatever because he wants all of them dead, and he offered me two million to help."

"Wait, you said Ghost?" Torey chimed in with a raised eyebrow.

"Yeah."

"Ghost from where?"

"He's too old for you to know, Torey. He's some old killa from Atlanta. Back in the days type shit. He randomly called my phone last night on some mystery shit and told me to meet up with him for a sit down. He's really just trying to use me as a face in order to get the person he hunting down at that table, and I think it's Richard and some bitch named Eva." Ryan rubbed his chin in think mode.

Torey sat back in silence, soaking in the small story before heading towards the door. "I'll be back. I gotta make a run to the eastside and check on Free. The nigga can't manage without me too long."

"Are you sliding back through?" Ryan questioned.

"Maybe. I gotta figure a few things out. If I do, I'll call first," he replied before closing the front door behind him.

"Ay, Ryan, I'm not gonna lie. I need to do the same. I gotta make my way to the west side and check on the headquarters too. My people ain't been shuffling right, and in order to keep this product pushing, we gotta inform people on what the hell is going on. I didn't expect to still be serving weight two months after the designated date, but I'm riding this shit out with you until you say we good." Nas dapped him and Freddie up with a brotherly handshake.

"Word. Just tap in," Ryan replied.

Demerea nodded towards Freddie, and he instantly got the message. Throwing the deuces quietly, he slid out of the house, and Demerea hit the locks behind him.

Ryan looked up at her when she flopped down on the couch next to him. "Is there anything I can do for you, daddy? I know you upset right now, but sitting around the house on edge won't help. I really feel like people want you to be down."

"It really doesn't matter, Demerea. Precious was a big part of me. She helped with everything I started. The shit doesn't even feel right without her. The club, the motivation. She was the fucking key." Ryan balled up his fist in anger, shaking it like a rock in a sock.

"Ryan. I understand that, and her genuine friendship will never be replaced because she was really special. That's why she knew what it took in order to push your talent out. She saw your vision. Am I right?" Demerea scooted closer to look into his eyes. "Ryan, you're a hustler that's about to take over this weak-ass game for the next six months, and after that, you will be one of the richest young nineteen-year-old's I know. You're strong, and Precious knew that. It's the reason you accomplished so much with her, and this will be the reason you accomplish the same with me. I'm holding you down, Ryan. I know you need it because real ones don't come a dime a dozen. My loyalty is here." Demerea pulled a pregnancy stick from her pocket and placed it into his hands. "We've been smashing for months unprotected, Ryan. I'm having yo' baby!" She kissed the side of his face like a kid was greater than his business associate dying.

Looking in her eyes, Ryan grabbed the test. "Are you serious? 'Cause I don't have time to play with you, Demerea. You only been staying with me for a week."

"Mm-hmm, and yo' ass been skeeting months before I came over here. Ryan, why did you always just come and hit me on a late night like I wasn't the Queen from the jump? I mean, I don't wanna keep bringing it up. But did it take that to really happen with Faith and Precious to see that I'm worthy and special too?"

Setting down the test with excitement, Ryan hugged her. "No, Demerea. It's just a certain way things work. All I wanted was a baby and a family of my own to take care of. Now my baby mama probably about to get a life sentence, and my son is in the custody of a lady who doesn't want me to see him ever again. It's not that you weren't worthy of being noticed. You played your position, and you won. It's simple. My only mission now is to get the money right and never look back again."

"Those were my thoughts exactly. Ryan, I'm not about to go through the same thing as Faith. That's why you need to run it up now and wrap it up. I can start helping you on the business side the same way. You know my dad is connected with a lot of people too," Demerea reminded him.

"I do remember, and I know we're gonna be good. I wonder what I'm having." He rubbed her belly with a smile.

"A baby girl. That's what I want. We don't need a son where you can grow him up on the same shit you know. See, if you have a daughter, that'll calm yo' ass down." She giggled.

"You may be right. I gotta get ready to meet this nigga at the club later on tonight. It shouldn't be for long, because I really wanna head out myself." He sat up, looking at the time.

"You should, Ryan. It's your birthday. "

"Yeah, that shit don't mean too much when you get older and see that ain't nothing special about it, besides you gaining some more wisdom. I'm trying to have the money to match that."

"I understand, boy, but it's a way to make that happen, Ryan. There is nothing greater than enjoying that moment with the ones you love also. We only get one life, and that shit so hard to keep. In order to move right, you have to want better." Demerea spilled him some real knowledge.

"True. Just make sure you find us something to do tonight. After I meet up with him at Club Royal tonight, I'm coming back to find us something to get into."

Ryan moved towards his room and jumped straight into the closet. Picking out some small fly shit, he laid it on the bed. A pair of Robin jeans. A Gucci shirt with the matching belt, and a new pair of Gucci kicks straight from the city of New York.

After showering and hopping fresh, Ryan sat around and kicked a little more shit with Demerea. Even though they had been sneaking around for only a few months, it felt like she was his main homie. She kept it more solid than a few of the niggas who were on the team. She wasn't cutting her tongue for anybody, and that right there was a true indication of a real one in his eyes. Not only was she quicker on her feet, but she had more history with the streets than Faith. She wasn't scared to get her feet wet and stand in the paint if something was going wrong. That was the reason Ryan decided to go ahead and keep her around. It was easy to find a bitch who wanted to lay around and be up under a nigga, but finding one who could match your hustle was rare.

After pouring out a few laughs with her ass, he stared at the clock and realized that he needed to get a headstart on getting to the club. There was no way he could fuck this million dollar deal up for anyone. After kissing Demerea, Ryan walked out of the house with his head up high. Even though Precious was lost, she didn't take her joy. She left him a cool-ass new chick, and exposed Faith's crooked ass. It didn't matter about anything else.

Ryan jumped into his truck and kissed the picture of Precious hanging around his mirror. She was the angel keeping him in order. Nothing could beat that love, and Ryan was about to prove that shit. After the money and deal were made, shit was about to go up. Fuck the King of Delaware. Ryan wanted the throne.

Chapter 11
Club Royal
8:25 p.m.

Ryan moved around the club, making sure that all the guests were having a great time. Ryan headed to the bar and snatched up a quick drink. The best move was signing the club over to Precious's family. Not only were they business people, but their connections for promotions were out of this world.

"Can I get one Patron?" Ryan asked the small-framed bartender behind the counter.

"Yes sir."

It didn't take long to spot the man after he remained seated for a while. He was surely easy to spot. He was dressed in all black, and his snapback lay gently over his eyes. The black trench coat he wore made him look like something out of a *Punisher* movie. That nigga Ghost had the perfect name. When he lifted his hand, Ryan knew for sure that it was him. He made his way towards the small reserved section. He was sitting in the corner by himself. A bottle of Hennessy was on the glass table, and a blunt of exotic was burning between his fingers.

"Young'un, it took you long enough. I thought I might have to expose myself in order for you to see me. That's definitely not how I move. "

The music was bumping, and people moved around like it was the best night of their lives. Ghost pointed at them all with a smirk. "It's funny to see these motherfuckers bounce around like ain't nothing at stake. People around this bitch dying daily, and this is what people like to do. Party." Ghost chuckled lightly.

"I mean, that's the way of the world, big dawg. It ain't that much killing and pain in somebody to move like that every day. Sometimes you gotta release that negative energy. I do it all the time." Ryan nodded while taking a sip of his drink.

"So is there anything new? No sign of the woman yet?" he asked, disregarding Ryan's statement.

"Nah, I been trying my best to get a little closer to Richard. He claims that I'm his best seller since a lot of people at the table been slacking. That actually might be the way in. Of course I heard him speak on the boss lady shit again, but still no sight of her. "

"Well, maybe you're not looking hard enough, little man. Eva isn't one who's meant to be seen. She's the one who will be ducking in the shadows waiting for people to move for her. The trick is to pay attention to the shit you can't see. Eva is not the average woman. She's my aunt, but her skills for moving are pro. She could be there the entire time without you knowing a thing. That's the reason I'm paying you." Ghost inhaled on the weed and passed it to Ryan.

"So you want me to look at shit that I don't usually pay attention to? Because there's not much going on in that bitch. It's a woman who works upstairs named Lizzy. She's a bartender. The two women who operate downstairs with Richard are like some fake-ass *Robocop* hoes. These bitches kill on instinct, and if Richard gives the order, yo' ass dead meat," Ryan verified.

Ghost yawned. "Those bitches are the least of my worries. That's anybody with a gun, for that matter. I am Death. I just want my target so I can make my way out of this slow-ass city. I'm too far away from home, and this is slowing me down. "

"How did you get my number?" Ryan asked curiously.

"The same way you went to a phone store and got you one assigned, dummy. If you gonna be working with me, there's a few things that you need to sharpen up with. I don't move sloppy, and you doing something so small could get a nigga crossed in the fire of some shit that you can't make it out of. I don't lose, young'un, and I'm not about to start now. When you walk, walk with confidence so a nigga will know not to second guess where you going. When you speak, talk with arrogance so a bitch won't ever think to play with you, even about the smallest shit. And when you bust that gun, shoot that bitch until you know that everything in your way is dead. That's how you move in this world. Anything opposite, and the Grim Reaper will be right there, ready to drag yo' ass off into the fire, li'l nigga."

Ryan soaked up the wise words from the real one and made sure to pay attention to every detail. Within twenty minutes, Ghost schooled him on the smallest to the biggest of things to be prepared for in the life of dirty-ass crime. Some people weren't built for shit like the world of envy and greed, but it came along with the way a street nigga lived. If I wasn't in you, the game was gonna swallow you alive as if you were never alive. Ryan also learned that just because you had paper or felt that being a killer was your best trait didn't mean that there wasn't somebody out there who could do it better. It was the reason why real killers didn't brag and boast. They just handled the business and left the rest for the news to figure out.

"So what's the new objective? Should I just call you when I see the woman and make shit easier?" Ryan suggested.

"Yeah, you should. That number is something I don't spread, so be careful how you operate with that line. I don't need the police calling me," Ghost said with a straight face.

"Never that." Ryan took out his phone and snapped a quick picture of him and the real deal mentor of the streets.

When Ghost spotted the flash, he grabbed Ryan's wrist. "Don't ever do that shit again. I don't do pictures. Period. This isn't a photo shoot, young'un. It's business. Stay focused." Rising off the couch, he looked down at Ryan. "I'll be in touch. But all you have to do is ring my line if that woman shows. I'll always be around. But just to make you aware, if she ever shows up and you make that call, try to get up out of there as quickly as possible, because when I come, nobody but me is leaving," Ghost said before disappearing out into the crowd of the club.

Ryan looked down at the glass table and spotted a small piece of folded paper. He picked it up and opened it, staring at the Virgin Island stamp on the front. It looked like a napkin from a bar or something, but it definitely wasn't shit from the States like Ryan was used to. Balling it up, he thought about the major game that was just dropped on him. It didn't take the smartest man in the world to know how to move with every problem. You just had to be smarter than any other men competing against you. Those little key pointers made him want to gain more info from the mysterious street nigga that came from out of nowhere.

After checking in with the runner of the club, Ryan headed out and jumped back into his truck. If Ghost wanted him to stick around until he spotted this bitch, then so be it. Richard was playing his games hard, but it didn't matter, because his ass was gonna still be popped in the end too. The only person who was doing any winning was Ryan, and that shit was a promise he was willing to die over, just like it was explained from the real killer himself.

His misconception of Ghost's words was something that Ryan didn't catch. The one thing he didn't know about the heartless devil was that his mind didn't care for anyone unless you were blood-related to him. It didn't matter if you lost your life or people died in the mix. It was his game of chess, and if you didn't play it accordingly, you were bound to see his face before you took your last breath.

Chris Green

Chapter 12
Ryan's spot, 10:04 p.m.

Jumping out of whip, Ryan looked up at the dark sky. The half-moon was shining brightly, and the wind was pushing harder now that it was getting down towards the bottom of the year. Ryan hit the alarm and headed up for the spot. Thinking about Demerea placed a small smile on his face. It actually felt good to get a girl pregnant that hadn't been slayed by one of his friends. The hurtful shit DJ pulled with Faith was something he never expected to pop up, but it was all a part of the game. But that's the reason why everything was gonna be strictly about paper from now on. If it wasn't, than it surely wasn't gonna make sense.

After placing his key inside the door, he stepped in and nearly pulled his strap once everybody screamed loudly.

"Happy birthday, Ryan!"

A small smile formed across his face when he spotted all of his high school friends in the building. Demerea was standing in the center looking sexier than ever in her strapless Fendi dress and heels. Numerous people walked over to him, embracing Ryan with hugs and gifts. After being bum-rushed by all his close associates and friends, Ryan grabbed Demerea in a full bear hug.

"Thank you, fathead. You was planning this the whole time, huh?" He looked into her face, flashing a handsome smile.

"Uh, duh. You know that I couldn't allow you to sit around here on your birthday depressed. Precious wouldn't want that either. So I called a few friends to come support you on your day. "

"Thanks, li'l mama. That really means a lot," Ryan said as he stared at everybody moving around with food plates and liquor cups. A huge cake was sitting on the table, and balloons were floating at the top of his ceiling, indicating the special day of his birth. Even though he wasn't much of a celebrator, it felt good to see a house full of people who truly had love for him.

Demerea whispered in his ear before he could walk off, "I have another surprise for you too." She smiled.

Ryan licked his lips, anticipating her gift. "Oh yeah? How you wanna handle that?"

Laughing, she slapped his shoulder. "That's for later, silly. Not that gift. I'm talking about her." She pointed at Kimyetta standing on the side of his living room wall.

Her face was bunched up with anger until she saw the big-ass kiddie smile that lit up Ryan's face. Moving past Demerea, he jolted over to her and lifted Kimyetta into the air. All Ryan could do was kiss her repeatedly.

"Boy, set me down before you drop me." She giggled with relief to see that he was still in one piece. There was no other pain like a mother grieving over her hard-headed son who just couldn't do right. Kimyetta couldn't step away from the house two minutes without someone claiming to have her child on some illegal shit. Here he was now nineteen and still being the bad-ass Ryan she birthed so long ago.

"Mama, why you ain't tell me you was coming to see me?" Ryan placed Kimyetta down on her feet.

"Because, I didn't know you was throwing a party. Demerea got in contact with me. You know, I heard about what happened. Do you see why I asked you to leave now?" She looked at him with an I-told-you-so face.

"I know, I know, Ma. I just ain't expect nothing like that to go down. Not with Faith anyway." His voice trailed off. He did not want to keep reliving that moment.

"It just goes to show you, Ryan. It don't matter who you feel we can trust in this world. Everybody has a breaking point where they could break and turn on you. It's not in our power to stop it everywhere, but we should always try to avoid it when we see that it's clear. Ain't shit here in Wilmington, and that's why I got the hell away from here. It took yo' daddy away from me, and I know you're bound to be next if shit like this keep going on." Kimyetta folded her arms sadly.

"Man, I know, Mama. You ain't gotta stress 'bout that no more. I already decided that I was leaving this shit for good. I got six more months to build up my paper, and then I'm moving you away for good. I can't make this a long term goal, and that's something I'm just now learning. Everybody grows. You just gotta give it a chance to soak in." Ryan grabbed her hand in a pleading manner.

"Uh huh. Who the hell you been talking to? 'Cause my son is a whole street thug. He don't know nothing 'bout shit like this." She checked Ryan's temperature to make sure his ass wasn't sick.

Laughing, he kissed her fingers. "Stop it, lady. It's me. I do have the right to get older and mature. I'm just evaluating a lot, and now I'm weighing my options on things. I'm tired of being away from you, and I'm sick of being around a bunch of motherfuckers that don't care about me. I'm glad you were able to make it to my party though. I feel like I haven't seen you in years. "

Chris Green

"Whatever. I ain't been gone that long. Next time I'ma stay away for a whole year and see how you feel then," Kimyetta threatened playfully.

"Don't make me go crazy, lady. That's not what I'm trying to hear right now. Remember, it's my birthday," he pleaded with a smirk.

"Mm-hmm. Go ahead and have some fun with your little friends. I'll be here overseeing y'all for a while to make sure things don't get out of control. You know y'all little asses need some parental guidance when y'all start smoking and getting drunk."

"I love you, Mama." He kissed her cheek and bobbed off through the crowd of friends that waited for him.

"A'ight. Now today's Ryan's birthday, so I would like everybody to please turn up to the max." Demerea cranked up the stereo.

The loud music erupted through the speakers, causing everyone to yell in excitement. Future's *56 Nights* quaked inside the four walls, instantly causing the teens to pour up. Weed was lit, and hot-ass young teens were popping coochie like it was the last night of freak'nik. The love was so great, but all Ryan could think about was Precious. She would've loved to be a part of his special day. There was nothing like a friend who could tell you everything you felt and wanted to do it by the sight of your face. Precious was a low-key mind reader. It was the reason Ryan couldn't deny her. Now that her love was gone, it was passed down to Demerea. She had the sex game on lock and the wifey traits of being humble and respectful. Plus she was a rider when it came down to him handling the business. It was sad to say, but everything that happened was meant to occur with them all, from the friends down to his relationship.

112

After an hour of straight partying, Ryan was having the time of his life. He was half past drunk. A blunt was burning for nothing in his hand because he damn sure wasn't smoking it, and the crowd was still growing by the minute.

The sound of the doorbell caused Demerea to break off from under Ryan's wasted ass to go and let the extra guest in. After making hot wings and burgers for the entire crib, she was finally exhausted and was close to shutting things down after that nigga wore himself out for a good night of sleep. Regardless of how tired he was, she was gonna be sure to bathe him, suck his dick until he came, and ride that dick into submission. That was gonna be reimbursement for all the loud-ass guests she gathered for his crazy ass.

Getting to the door, Demerea opened it to see DJ standing on the other side. Her face frowned in disappointment. "Uh, was he expecting you?"

"Bitch, get the fuck out of my way. I came to see my dawg for his birthday. Plus I gotta tell him some important shit. Does he know that you a slime-ass female?" DJ spat back with an attitude. It wasn't like him to spazz out on the regular, but there was just something not sitting right with Demerea. After being Faith's friend for years, she got involved in the incident with Precious, and she just turned her back on Faith as if they were never close. Not even a few weeks of her being away, and she was sleeping with Ryan like they were a married couple. It was disgusting in his eyes, and she was a snake that couldn't be trusted.

Stepping to the side, Demerea flashed a sly smile and allowed him to enter. "Go right ahead then, big man."

DJ brushed passed her and headed straight over to the small crowd where Ryan stood. It didn't take long before the small room grew quiet after the two eyes met since their last incident. DJ knew how Ryan could get, so he took the initiative to start off the conversation.

"Wassup, bro? I need to really chop it up with you about some important shit."

"Important?" Ryan slurred. "Nigga, what's more important than my motherfuckin' birthday? I'm drinking, smoking, and enjoying my real friends. It ain't shit else to talk about besides that."

The surrounding guests looked at DJ as if he was a buzzkill. Everyone knew about the recent confrontation between him and Ryan, which had left the men beefing with each other. It was a slap in the face to most people they had known since middle school. Everyone knew that Faith was only for Ryan, and vice versa. That small secret was dividing their friendship and even other people from embracing him.

"Ryan, I know you're mad, bro. But it's some serious shit going on right now. I need to tell you this," DJ pleaded.

"Cut the fucking radio off. Cut it off!" Ryan yelled, causing everybody to stop moving. The loud music eventually came down to a low volume.

Kimyetta could see that her son was about to start some trouble and decided to make her way over to him.

"Listen up, y'all. This nigga DJ got something to tell me. I don't know why you wanna make it all a quiet conversation now, nigga. Tell everybody. Tell all of them how you fucked my baby mama, nigga. That's what you wanna talk about, right?" Ryan pointed an unsteady finger at him.

"Ryan, you need to chill the fuck out. You causing a scene, bro." DJ was noticing how all the attention in the room was now on him.

"I ain't calming shit down. You fucked my girl, pussy-ass nigga. You was supposed to be my boy. Now I'm guessing you wanna come and apologize, huh? Well, guess what I ain't accepting of, nigga? You crooked, and everybody in this bitch knows now. "

Kimyetta grabbed the cup from Ryan's hand and tried to make him sit down in a chair. Instead of obliging, he continued to take shots.

"I had love for you, nigga. That was, until you fucked my bitch."

"I told you that shit happened before you, nigga! Let it go. This is the reason I didn't want to tell you, because you act like a female when you're in your feelings," DJ snapped. He was tired of being embarrassed in front of all their people without standing up for himself. It was the last straw.

"Nigga, what? You the female, lame-ass nigga." Ryan struggled to get free from Kimyetta.

"Ryan, calm down," she said, holding his arms to keep him back.

"All I wanted to do was let you know the shit that's being said in the street, nigga. We boys, and you act like that shit don't mean nothing. I could've been fake and allowed niggas to keep talking greasy about you, but I pulled up because I'm your friend, nigga!"

"Fuck friends! I don't care about that shit, bitch-ass nigga. I'm me. That's all I need is me. I'll kill you, DJ." Ryan pushed Kimyetta off of him. The force caused her head to slam against the glass table behind her.

The action caused DJ to punch Ryan, sending him to the floor. Jumping on top of him, he placed another lick to his right jaw. As they tussled, a few of Ryan's guests grabbed DJ off of him and started to jump his ass like the old days. Four niggas punched and kicked on him until they got him towards the front door. The small get together that had started off great turned into a disaster, and mayhem was starting to break out. Ryan raised off the floor and pulled a gun from his hip. Luckily Nas was there beside him to grab it and hold him down.

Demerea shut off the music and screamed at the top of her lungs, "Everybody get out. Get out! The party is over."

A few of Ryan's friends helped Kimyetta off the floor and guided her to the couch to take a seat while Ryan fussed to be let loose.

The small group of men threw DJ out of the apartment on his face with Demerea directly behind them. She looked down at him trying to catch his breath.

"I warned you not to come in. Look what you've caused, DJ. This isn't a place for you to call anyone a friend. You came and ruined Ryan's birthday, and now you're no longer welcome," she spat before walking back into the crib and slamming the door.

Allowing his adrenaline to settle down, DJ picked himself up off the ground. Wiping the small line of blood from his lip, DJ smirked. "I hope yo' dumb ass can dodge death, idiot!" he shouted from outside of the door.

Trailing off down the small steps, DJ headed to his car and climbed inside. After starting the engine, DJ slammed a hand down on his dashboard. The pain of his friend not listening was more hurtful than a fight could ever weigh on him. There was only one way that a nigga like Ryan would listen, and it wouldn't happen until he was trapped in a cold box under a pile of six feet dirt.

Chris Green

Chapter 13
7:55 a.m.

After pulling up to the front of Ryan's Philly apartment, Markie-D stepped out of his small Honda Accord and moved towards his front door. He knocked lightly and waited patiently for an answer. No movement could be heard on the other side, but the sight of Ryan's Infiniti truck was enough clarification that he was probably inside. After knocking two more times, he stepped back and waited again.

The sound of locks adjusting grabbed his attention and Demerea opened the door with one of Ryan's T-shirts covering her body. Rubbing her eyes, she mugged Faith's old-ass daddy. "Markie-D, what are you doing here?"

"Hey Demerea. I was wondering if Ryan was home."

"How did you find this house? Did Faith tell you where he lived? Because he's not really accepting random pop ups," she confirmed with a slight attitude.

"I'm sorry, Demerea. Are you Ryan's girlfriend or something now? Because the last time I checked, he was crawling up my daughter's ass, sweetheart. Can you please show some respect for yourself by putting on some clothes and letting Ryan know that I'm here to speak with him please? I would really appreciate it."

Smacking her teeth, she closed the door in his face.

Markie-D knew that when it came to the young teens today, they had no respect for any elders. There was a form of respect that he always tried to teach Faith, to show respect until someone disrespected and the ability to protect herself if it came down to it, but to only use it if shit was necessary. The only thing he could try and do

119

was offer his piece of mind and allow the rest to flow as it came.

After a few minutes of waiting around, Ryan stepped out on the front porch with a rolled blunt in his mouth. A Glock 40 pistol hung from his pocket, and from the looks of it, the right side of his jaw was slightly swollen.

"How the hell did you find my spot, old head? I'm really not kicking it right now, Markie-D." Ryan sparked his joint and stood back against the door frame.

"What happened to your face?"

"Nun I couldn't handle. Why are you here is the question, old head?" Ryan shot back.

Markie-D exhaled and nodded. "The reason I'm here is on behalf of my daughter."

"There ain't nobody I wanna talk to about that," Ryan hissed.

"Hey now, I been knowing you since you were a kid, young blood. You mean to tell me it ain't no respect left in yo' bones for an OG like me? Yeah, you and my daughter didn't link until middle school, but me and your dad were tight as thieves when you were still in the nutsack, Ryan. That has to count for something, li'l bull. You ain't got shit to prove for me. I'm asking you to do it for them. Show me a little respect, young bull. Put that shit out and listen to me for five minutes."

Hearing the wise man's words, Ryan knew that his name truly did hold weight. Markie-D wasn't just a well-respected hood nigga. He was a legend when it came down to the street shit, the real father of the hood who was willing to stand up for every child, no matter who your biological father was.

After tapping the blunt against the doorframe, Ryan folded his arms. "I'm listening."

"Ryan, you've loved my daughter for years, and you now have a handsome young son that became your responsibility when you got her pregnant. Now I know that she isn't perfect, but Faith ain't gonna hurt nobody if they haven't harmed her. My baby is sitting behind a cell for a crime that she didn't commit. Now I'm not saying it's your responsibility, but it's a duty that you should perform on the strength of your son. She needs help with a lawyer, and I've already given all I could. You're her last resort, and that's the reason I'm on your doorstep today."

"Look, Markie, no disrespect, but Faith took somebody away from me that I truly cared for. Her attitude and actions placed her in that spot, and now when she's in a bad predicament, her conscience has kicked in. Faith is on her own with that." Ryan shook his head with regret.

"If that's the way you feel, son, I can't make you feel any different. I'm just gonna say this last thing, and I'll be on my way. This girl that you lost, have you ever taken the time to place that same effort into my daughter? Because I know my baby girl, and no matter how much I told her to be careful with you, she told me that you were destined to be with her. The nights where I had to comfort her for your mistakes, or all the times that she gathered up her last dollar to pay off some dumb shit you did… Why would a woman like that wanna take anything else from you after you throw that to the ground as if it's nothing?"

"What about Ms. Anderson? She turned Faith in for a reward, and no one is saying shit about that. Ten thousand dollars, Markie-D. Obviously she feels like her daughter did it," Ryan stated.

121

"And do you see that bitch right here with me now? No, Ryan, you don't. Faith's mom has a drug problem, and we've known that for years. She's tried to cover that up for years, and that was the only way she felt that Faith could stay away from you. Think about it, son. This girl who you lost… You've let her twist your head up so bad that you've forgotten about the ones who would be willing to lay down their all for you. One of those people is my baby girl. No matter how much you down her, no matter how much you dismiss her calls, she had your son. My grandson. That means family, Ryan, and family is always before anything. I guess after you started making all that bread, none of that matters, huh?" Markie-D said before walking off his doorstep.

Ryan couldn't help but sit back and dwell on those deep words. Faith was his queen at a point of time, the one who would break a back or fight any bitch at Newark to make sure her spot was secured. She was the one he felt never could do any wrong. But the day he lost Precious placed a different vision in his mind of her. No one in this world would harm a sweet innocent spirit like her for any apparent reason, and that's what gave him the right to feel the way he did. Faith was the only person who had been talking greasy about harming her, the only one who wanted to fight just because Precious was being a true friend. She did her dirty deed, and now she was looking for a way out. Unfortunately, that way couldn't come from Ryan.

Chapter 14
Female maximum security pod
Three months later

Black Girl was on her fifteenth round of squats, and Faith was directly behind her. After the last few months of studying her case, learning a new language, and soaking up great knowledge from Black Girl, Faith decided to accept the fact that jail was her current position and there was no other choice but to deal with it. Her mother, of course, made it seem to the authorities that she was too dangerous for Prince to be around her. The visitation was denied, and also the rights to custody were denied until after trial. Mr. Jeff Hovecek was keeping Faith aware about the small payments her dad made constantly every week with his paychecks. He was willing to give every coin, even if that meant him going homeless in order to see his daughter free again. Still, after giving up everything he had, Markie-D made sure that she could at least make the commissary list every week.

After being taken under Black Girl's wing, Faith truly didn't want for anything. Her box was always loaded with extra store and hygiene. Black Girl would order her clothes monthly and was sure to slap any bitch unconscious who disrespected her with any pettiness. Faith actually had become fond of the 6'2'' beauty. Her tongue game was like fucking mind control, and after three months of being caged in the room with her, the fetish became repetitive. What started off as an ass beating led to pleasure and moans every night they were locked behind the steel door. The sight of how much a girl could please her made the hate for men grow in Faith quickly, especially that fuckboy Ryan. The word of him and Demerea being in a relationship crushed her fucking heart to pieces. She even made an effort to call him, but was rejected every time. It was scary how Demerea wouldn't answer her letters or respond back to the messages Faith sent through mutual friends. It was clear that she had been crossed out, and that shit was building a stone heart in Faith daily.

After doing her fifteenth set, Faith jumped up. "What do you think?" She smirked seductively at Black girl. Within three months of straight workout, her ass was on swole and her tummy was smaller than a track swimmer's. Faith was already slim, but the thickness added onto her frame was a major plus.

Black Girl smiled. "It looks like you trying to get yo ass folded up and ate to pieces." She slapped her butt lightly.

"Later, freak." She giggled before grabbing her things to shower. "So I was thinking about my case and what these people were trying to offer me. The last court date, the district attorney tried to force fifteen years. He said if I don't take it, then I'm bound to get a life sentence at trial. What do you think I should do?"

"You ain't taking shit, Faith, because you ain't did shit. I've been going over your shit myself, and it's straight trash. The only problem is how your gun came back positive from forensics on killing her. We have to tighten that up, because that alone makes you look guilty. Who is close enough to get your gun and do some shit like that? Because that's what we will have to figure out first. It's a delicate situation when it comes down to a murder case."

"There's a couple of people, but my friend Demerea - well, the bitch I thought was my friend - knew where it was. But she wasn't around me that night besides at the party. I left her house and went home, and the gun was still there. That's why it's a mystery to me. I can't remember shit. It's like I was drugged," Faith admitted.

"How do you know that you weren't?

Faith shrugged. "I guess I never looked at it that way."

"Well, guess what? You have to. We can ask your lawyer to run a test from your blood the night it was taken when you were booked in. If something was in your bloodstream, we can continue the investigation further than what the district attorney is trying to take it." Black Girl waved her finger in think mode.

Faith began to think to herself before sitting in the bed next to Black Girl. "Can I ask you something?

"Sure."

"When you killed your husband, how did it feel?"

"What do you mean?" Black Girl flashed a curious expression.

"Like what did it make you feel like? Was it hard for you to do it?" Faith stammered over her words, not trying to be so direct.

Black Girl gazed out of the medium-sized window for a second before answering. "To be honest, it felt good. There's nothing like a man scorning a woman who's in love. I gave him everything in my power. My money, my heart, my body. It was a point in time where I didn't even want to be around my mother because she always told me to leave him. She claimed there was an evilness she sensed inside of him. Of course I didn't believe it because I was so wrapped around his finger. That day I came home and saw a bitch riding his dick and it sent me over the edge. So I killed his ass, and it felt good." Black Girl smirked with no regret.

"So what if I feel the same way you do?" Faith asked seriously.

"That's something you have to figure out for yourself, baby. You're similar to me. Like my little widow. We weren't meant to be a man's wife. Let me explain this, and you can judge it how you please after I'm done. A man who cares, who truly cares, he wouldn't ruin something worth a lifetime for some shit that's only temporary. You have men who make mistakes, but what truly is a mistake in your eyes? If you ask me, it ain't no such thing as mistakes, because I'm either enough for you or I'm not. If you choose to do anything other than be a King for me, then you've wasted your time, and that gives me the authority to show how you fucked up. I'll cut a nigga's dick off. Slash a nigga's throat. Do whatever it takes for you to understand that a bitch's heart ain't just a toy. It's the reason I love women. Because nobody can feel a bitch's pain like another woman who's been hurt. Do you get what I'm saying?" Black Girl schooled her.

"Yeah." Faith lowered her head. "So if I got out, and got my revenge on these people, would I be wrong?"

"I can't say that you would be wrong about anything unless you don't do it for a purpose. Revenge is cool, but there has to be more. Anybody can upset you, Faith. What will you do, kill everybody after that?"

"I mean, no, but I was crossed out by a lot of people, and hell yeah, that shit hurts, but I don't wanna kill everybody. I just want them to feel my pain. What other purpose is there?"

Black girl smiled wickedly. "Power."

* * *

Severe and Teona

7:45 p.m.

As he drove the raggedy junkie rental down DJ's street, Severe cursed himself for ever getting involved with a bitch when it came down to business. For months they had been laying outside of DJ's spot waiting for Ryan to appear. They even spent days following him, and still hadn't come across the man even once. Detective Bradley was lurking, hassling Severe about the funds he paid for Ryan's head. Also, the info he spilled to him about the table would cost his life if he didn't make good on the deal that they had agreed upon. It was beyond Severe's knowledge that Ryan had relocated deeper into Philadelphia.

Severe looked over at Teona fanning herself in the passenger seat. "How long do you think we about keep doing this shit? We been sliding over here every week for the past two in a half months, and still haven't seen this man yet. This can't be the only fucking plan you got?"

"Severe, you the one who trying to be low key and hide from the police, motherfucker. We could've been caught this nigga if you wouldn't have tried to stay ducked off in a damn hotel worrying about this man. How can he expect ya to find this man if he keeps threatening to do something to you!" she snapped with an agitated manner.

"Bitch, calm the fuck down. I just asked a question. We dealing with some real fucking people here, and I'm not trying to die."

"Duh, nigga, neither am I. You said that you were gonna handle this nigga on the strength of my sistas, remember? You the one dragging me around all day with you," she called out his bullshit.

"Yeah, and I also offered yo' broke ass protection, and money too. Don't forget about that. You were just broke without ya sisters little robbing check feeding yo' ass. I been supporting you, dummy, and don't forget that I'm the same nigga who's getting a million dollars out of this shit," Severe bragged like he already had possession of the large check.

"Whateva, Severe."

Their silence fell strong for a few minutes until she spotted the all-black Infiniti truck pulling down DJ's street. "Nigga, that's him. It's Ryan." She pointed at the truck.

Severe shivered. "Chill, chill. Just let me see to be sure." He ducked down as the truck pulled in front of the home.

Chapter 15

Driving down the street in his new black Infiniti Q6, DJ smiled with joy. After all the time he spent away from Ryan, his boy finally came back to his senses. It was a blessing to tighten things up with Ryan after their major fight. Things were being said in the streets, and of course dirty-ass motherfuckers were slandering names left and right about who was saying what. Still and all, they were able to reconnect and squash their differences once the mission about the money became clear. Friends were going to argue, but there was never supposed to be a separation to the point where the bond was no longer there. True friends were surely what they were because the two were back on track.

It was a blessing for DJ to get a call from Princeton University the day before. His acceptance papers were reviewed by the professor of his studies, and they offered to let him enter school a few months early to receive a head start with the college graduates who were about to exit into the big world. Tomorrow was that big day, and after Ryan found out, DJ woke up to the blessing of a new whip to leave in style. It was just like Ryan's, but better. He even threw in a brand new, updated Chromebook computer for the proper research and schoolwork that would be approaching him. Now that he was back in tune with his main man, it was time to put the Delaware life behind him. No one could ever have the nerve to say that niggas from Wilmington wasn't gonna be shit. It wasn't average to hear about a young nigga straight out of Newark making it into Princeton.

It was almost eight o'clock at night, and shit was just getting started. It was the last moment in Delaware he was gonna remember, so DJ wanted to end it with a little fun. Ryan was taking him and the team out for drinks and to pop a little shit in Club Royal. Ever since Precious's little sister signed the papers to take over, she had spruced that bitch up to the max. Ryan was still receiving a percentage off of everything being made, plus he had established a personal account for Prince whenever his fuck-ass granny decided to get off the bullshit. Shit was finally laced, and now it was time to part ties with his old neighborhood.

After pulling down his street, DJ parked in front of his mother's home. Tossing the black hoodie over his head, he stepped out into the cutting wind. January was about to get hectic and it felt good to be whipping in some nice shit to stay warm.

The sound of a car door closing made him jerk slightly. He wanted to turn around, but the harsh wind forced him to keep it pushing. His heart nearly froze when he heard the voice behind his neck breathing like a rabid dog.

"I told you, li'l nigga, you couldn't hide forever!"

DJ swung his body around to meet the face that greeted him. Four shots rang out quickly.

Boom! Boom! Boom! Boom!

DJ never felt the bullets collide with his face. His body collided against the pavement, knocking his hoodie off in the process. Severe moved to place another slug into his face, but paused in shock once he realized that it wasn't Ryan.

"Oh shit! No! No!" He grabbed the side of DJ's head as the blood started to pour from the top of DJ's head and face.

The porch lights of the neighbors' houses began to fly on back to back. A distant dog began to bark, and at that point, Severe knew that he just made one of the worst mistakes ever.

Running back to the car, he jumped in, looking at Teona before speeding off.

"What? Why the hell are you acting so nervous? You did it." Teona looked behind them to make sure shit was clear if anyone was trying to follow them.

Severe continued to drive mumbling the same shit. "No! No!"

"Boy, what the fuck is wrong with you? Was that your first time or something?" she questioned with worry.

"That wasn't Ryan," he stammered

"What? What you mean that wasn't Ryan? He's the one who drives a black Infiniti truck like that. That's him."

"Teona, that was DJ," he admitted with worry.

The stupid look she gave him said it all. "What do you mean that was DJ? You was up on him. You already know how DJ looks, so how could you get them confused, Severe?"

"Bitch, it was DJ. He had a fucking hoodie on. The hoodie made him look different," he stuttered up another lie.

"Oh my God!" She covered her eyes. "If Ryan finds out we did that, we're gonna fucking die, nigga."

"No duh, bitch! You think he gonna still come around to a fucking crib where his best friend was just murdered?" he replied angrily while mashing the gas pedal.

"Calm down. No one has to know. It's not like anybody saw us, Severe. Me and you are the only two who know. We can still wait and handle Ryan when he appears for answers. Simple. That nigga ain't invincible." Teona gave him a confident look.

Severe nodded nervously. After geeking on cocaine and alcohol for the past month, his mind grew paranoid instantly, and he was bound to start beating the hell out of Teona on some straight spazz out shit. Knowing what could calm his nerves, she rubbed his thigh as he drove.

"Trust me. Plus this will give Bradley some type of confirmation that you really out here looking for this nigga. He'll respect that. That kills two birds with one stone, and it puts us closer to the money." She tried to build his confidence. Unzipping his pants, she removed his dick. "Just relax and think about what you gonna say to Bradley. The rest is gonna work out; watch." She smiled before placing her face into his lap. Wrapping her lips around his piece, she bobbed her head, making him go stiff quickly.

Severe exhaled when her warm mouth touched his dick. That shit was always his stress reliever. The shit she said definitely made sense. With Ryan's little best friend dead, he had less room to move around as freely as he wanted. Detective Bradley wouldn't have any choice but to respect that move until he applied the pressure on locating the big fish.

Looking down at Teona laying her head game down, Severe grunted lightly. She was the real one when it came down to making him comfortable, and that was the same reason he was gonna make sure she was straight also.

Taking her advice, he picked up his cell, and dialed Detective Bradley's number. He listened to it ring in his ear and then the line was picked up.

"This better be good. I haven't heard from you in a long time," Bradley's voice spoke calmly through the receiver.

"It is. I'm not done just yet, but you will like what's going on. I need to meet you so we can talk."

"Good. I'll see you tomorrow. Be looking for my call," Detective Bradley said before ending the call.

When Severe tossed the phone in the cup holder, Teona stopped her blowjob, looking up at him. "What did he say?"

"It's good."

"I told you." She smiled.

"Facts," was his only reply before guiding her face back to work.

Shit was about to get real with the paper flow if Detective Bradley agreed to the mission that he was prepared to go on, even if that meant him laying into Ryan's ass at DJ's funeral. One way or the other, Severe wasn't stopping until that mil ticket was in the bag.

* * *

9:34 a.m.
Wilmington Detention Center

As the hot sun grazed his face, Wicked smiled. It had been a long seven months of pain and misery after losing his cousin. His family in Arizona totally abandoned him once they found out about the fate of Reckless. His mother and aunt were big on family and since he was incarcerated, the blame was placed on him, especially since he was the oldest.

Taking the brown paper bag of property, he tossed it into the nearest trash can and tapped on the window of a taxi driver that was sitting in front of the institution.

"Where you need to go, man?" The African man rolled down the window and looked at Wicked's nappy hair with a crazy expression.

"The east side." He smiled with a devilish grin before jumping in the backseat.

It didn't take longer than twenty-five minutes before Wicked reached the east side of Delaware. After viewing the city and getting a whiff of the new fresh breeze, he was able to collect his thoughts on what he needed to do. Shit was out of tune on his behalf, and since motherfuckers wanted to take his flesh and blood, he was gonna take back all the shit Reckless wanted for keeps - starting off with Ryan.

He made the cab driver drop him off at the top of Torey's block. Wicked walked through the treacherous neighborhood with a bright smile. It was easy to spot a north side nigga on the wrong side of town. There was a smell that an east side nigga couldn't miss. The beef since the sandbox had been so real that younger cats who weren't even in the mix yet were raised to hate these niggas.

Trailing down the dead end street, Wicked stopped in front of Torey's driveway, where Free stood with six of their shooters. The men pulled their pistols as they watched Wicked stare them down as if he was crazy.

"You want me to kill this fool, Free?" one of the men whispered in his ear.

Waving him off, Free smiled and walked over to Wicked slowly. "You must have some big nuts coming down into this hood without a gun, nigga."

Wicked watched as he extended his hand, waiting for Free to come to him to shake it. Smiling, he pulled Free in for a brotherly hug. "What else do I got to lose, nigga? After all, why wouldn't I come and scream at the nigga who been looking out for me my entire bid? You even made sure I got out a few months early. That was a blessing, my guy. "

Free nodded and pulled out five hundred dollars. "Put that in ya pocket for right now. You look like an old-ass man with that beard and the hair on top of your head. You wanna clean up or something?"

"Nah, but what you can do is give me a burner. I'm out here tonight, and I ain't got no time to waste," Wicked said with a straight face.

Free pondered his request and slid the black and chrome 9mm handgun from his hip. Placing it in Wicked's hand, he shrugged. "Cool, but tonight is your first night. You sure you ain't tryna have no fun before you just go out here and start searching for Mr. Delaware?"

Wicked smirked with arrogance. "I'm Mr. Delaware," he stated before walking off.

Chris Green

Chapter 16

The loud sound of banging erupted on Ryan's front door, causing him to jump up. Demerea was the first to hop up.

"Whoever this is got some motherfucking nerve this early in the morning."

Ryan rubbed the corner of his eyes, trying to peep the time on his cell phone. After DJ never showed up to the club last night, he had tossed back a few drinks and headed back to the crib. It was already late in the evening, and it was probably him giving his farewells and goodbyes to all the loved ones.

Flicking on the front screen to his cell phone, Ryan stared at the thirty missed call notifications. "What the fuck?" he mumbled to himself

Before he could check it, Demerea crept back through the room quickly. "Ryan. It's like ten police officers at the door looking for you!" she whispered with her hands moving in the air.

"What? Did you open the door?" He jumped up from under the covers.

"Yes. I didn't think it was the damn police." She shook nervously. "What the hell did you do, boy?

"I ain't did shit. I don't even know how they found me," Ryan whispered before throwing on a pair of sweats. The one thing he knew was if they didn't come kicking in the door, then he obviously hadn't done shit wrong.

Ryan stepped out into his living room. He opened the front door, looking out at the group of officers aligned on his front porch. One of them quickly moved to the front in order to address him.

"Mr. Royal, is it possible you can come speak with us down at our station, please? Something has occurred, and we need to ask you a few questions. "

"Something like what? I ain't did shit. So whatever y'all got going on, you can speak about it right here if I'm not under arrest." Ryan folded his arms when Demerea walked up behind him.

The officer looked down and huffed before giving him the news. "We're trying to see what took place last night in Wilmington. Darius Miller was murdered in front of his mother's home, and she said if we find you, then we could find the problem."

Ryan stepped out of the doorway. Ryan's heart nearly collapsed upon hearing DJ's last name. "What the fuck did you just say?"

The officer repeated himself. "Your friend Darius Miller was murdered last night in front of his mother's home."

Demerea placed a hand over her mouth before Ryan punched the side of his door. "Fuck! Tell me you fucking lying, man. Tell me you lying!" he screamed outrageously in the officer's face.

Sensing that he was hurt, the officer grabbed one of his shoulders. "I'm sorry, Mr. Royal, but I'm not lying. This is the reason we're here this morning, to see if we can get your help. "

"What do you need me to do, man?" Ryan dropped his head in defeat as the tears cascaded down his cheeks.

"Just come down to the precinct and speak with us for a second. We can drop you right back off as soon as we're done."

Ryan looked back at Demerea. He rubbed her plump stomach, and kissed her. "Call my lawyer, and tell him to get down to the station. Don't answer the door for anyone," he ordered before heading down the stairs with the group of officers.

The news of DJ dying was about to wake the entire city of Delaware. The pain of his best friend dying a day before his admission into Princeton was a feeling that he would never be able to shake. It didn't matter what it took or how much it cost. Whoever made the grave mistake of murdering DJ was about to bring the old beast back to Wilmington once again, and Ryan wanted answers.

***

West side of Wilmington
Nas's apartment
11:21 a.m.

Nas sat up on his bed. He stared at the headline news on the TV in shock. "COLLEGE STUDENT MURDERED". The pain quickly rushed to his chest once he spotted DJ's name. He could only imagine how his mother felt. There wasn't any other feeling like losing your son in the nasty streets of Delaware a day before he started classes at one of the greatest schools in the United States. The shit was on every blog, every morning station, and every social media press.

After waking up early in the a.m., he received a call from Freddie about the incident and tried to alert Ryan, but never got an answer. Now, after finally getting Demerea to pick up the phone, she gave him the info about the police snatching up Ryan this morning out of his Philadelphia apartment. Shit was really insane, and at that moment, Nas didn't know what the fuck to do.

The sound of his doorbell broke his attention, causing him to rise from the bed and head for his living room. The doorbell sounded again before he could open it up. Once Wicked's and Nas's eyes met, fear took over him.

"Wicked, what are you doing at my house? I thought you were booked on a bid?"

"I was, but obviously they let me go. You gonna let me in, or do I gotta keep standing out here in this fuck-ass cold?" he asked with agitation in his tone.

Nas stepped to the side, allowing him to enter, locking the door behind him. He watched as Wicked took a seat on the couch.

"So what brings you to the west side? Does Ryan know you're home?" He sparked the cigarette sitting behind his right ear.

"Nah, you the only person right now. I didn't come over here to worry about me though. I just wanted to ask you a few questions about some shit." Wicked's hands were clutched inside his jacket pockets.

"What do you mean by *questions*?" Nas looked at him suspiciously. It had been three months since Ryan spoke on Wicked's name and him popping up out of the blue means that he was obviously snooping around to see what he could get his hands into.

"You know what I mean, Nas. My fucking cousin was killed, and I wanna know did you hear anything about it?"

"Reckless?" Nas said before inhaling on his cigarette.

"Exactly."

Shaking his head, Nas looked Wicked in the eyes, and lied. "Nah, bro. I haven't heard nothing about what happened to him, but I know that he was on the bullshit with some niggas from the east side. He was running around Wilmington like a fucking mad dog. I know that he got into it with Ryan about some money or something. He even dissed DJ. I can't say that I know exactly what he was going through, but I know he was out of control," Nas said with a nod.

"So you mean to tell me that ain't nobody heard about Ryan having Reckless murdered?" Wicked sat up straight on the couch. His eyes were scanning Nas for any sign of lies. You could always smell a snake, especially when it was one working with the king cobra himself.

"What? Nigga, you sound stupid. Ryan would never do no shit like that. Reckless's dumb ass got bodied outside of a fucking police station. That was a real deal personal beef, Wicked. Ryan has been out here making money and living. Reckless shot at this man, and he still tried to conversate and offer him a place on the team. We can't even think stupid like that, because I been around the entire time, bro. Whatever Reckless did, it was personal shit that he created on the outskirts of the northside."

"Bullshit!" Wicked spat before removing the pistol from his jacket pocket. Placing one in the chamber, he looked at Nas's pupils dilate. "How about I ask you one more time, nigga. This time I'll be a little clearer. Ryan and my cousin were beefing hard. I know because he told me that him and DJ pulled guns on him twice before he ended up dead. This the same bitch-ass nigga you working for. I don't wanna hurt you, Nas, but I will. Tell me what the fuck happened to my cousin."

Knowing that Wicked was dead serious. Nas tried to calm himself. The barrel of his gun was aimed straight for him, but his gun was sitting on the edge of his bed frame. Nas didn't want to make the wrong move, but there was no other option. When he broke for the room, Wicked jumped from the couch and fired a shot directly into his back.

Crashing to the floor, Nas gasped in pain.

"Motherfucker, y'all thought I was stupid, huh?" Wicked screamed loudly. "I told all y'all niggas that I was gonna come and kill every last one of ya." He was now standing over Nas as he crawled slowly in the hallway. Blood was pouring profusely from his back.

Wicked used his foot to flip Nas over. Nas was petrified, and he knew that today would be the last moment he spent on earth when the barrel aimed for his face.

"Don't look scared now, nigga. You should have thought before you tried to protect Ryan. Now you about to die and he's next," Wicked spat before plugging his ass three more times.

After watching Nas's soul disperse from the flesh, Wicked tucked the gun inside of his pants and headed for the door. Stepping outside, Wicked saw a uniformed officer heading straight for Nas's apartment. The blood on Wicked's shirt caused him to pause and reach for his gun.

"Sir, we heard gunshots. Is everything okay around here?"

Wicked knew that his chances were slim to none, and cooperating was the last thing on his mind. He reached for the gun on his waist.

The officer pulled his weapon. "Freeze!"

Before the gun could slide off Wicked's hip, two bullets pierced his chest, killing him instantly. His body fell back against Nas's apartment door and the officer moved swiftly over to him, kicking the gun across the breezeway. He looked down into Wicked's soulless eyes. He grabbed his radio and placed the call for backup.

Chapter 17

"Just like I told y'all before. The only reason my name is on the car is because of the business I own. The car was a graduation gift. The dope you found in that bitch was obviously his. He sells dope. Not me," Ryan explained to the officer to save his own ass.

The one kilo of cocaine he placed in the trunk of DJ's new whip was only until he made his way back down into Philly. It was discovered once the authorities checked the vehicle for evidence. The shit was so messy that DJ's mom kept proclaiming that Ryan was a drug lord and a murderer. She was the only reason he was sitting in the interrogation room of a fucking police station at the time. Ryan still couldn't accept the fact that his best friend was now dead.

The interrogating officer rose to his feet once the lieutenant of the department stepped in. "Williams. The kid's lawyer is here. Time's up. We have a situation out on the west side. We gotta move out now!"

"Yes sir."

Turning back around to face Ryan, he moved closer to be sure that his words were kept just between them two. "I know that you have something to do with this kid's death. I also know that you're a fucking drug dealer. I'm gonna hunt you down and make sure you spend the rest of your life in prison. You're free to go, Mr. Royal," he said with hatred in his tone.

Standing to his feet, Ryan gave him a confident look. "Try finding the right motherfucker that killed my friend and stop worrying about me, sir. That shit could be bad for your health. "

Heading out of the small room, Ryan's eyes landed on the officer who he never expected to see again: Mr. "Lock 'em the fuck up". Watching the weird-looking white cop mug him down, Ryan shook his lawyer's hand and was escorted quickly out of the station.

* * *

Ryan's spot, one hour later

Pacing back and forth, Ryan watched as Demerea moved around the crib and bagged up the last of their things. Freddie and Torey sat around the living room in silence. The murder of DJ struck everyone hard, especially when it was supposed to be his first day of school. No one knew how things were about to play out, but Ryan was definitely prepared to kill whoever and place the check where it was necessary for the sake of his friend's blood being shed.

"Has anyone heard from Nas yet?" Ryan questioned.

"Nah, I called his ass a thousand times. He just spoke to me this morning, but that was the last phone call," Freddie informed him.

"Something ain't sitting right around this motherfucker. Ain't no way that I lose my brother overnight, and now this nigga just disappears off the scene. My mind is going into overdrive, and I'm really about to snap. Freddie, I need you to pull up on that nigga and see what the fuck he got going on. If his ass ismoving fishy, get rid of him today," Ryan ordered.

144

Freddie shrugged his shoulders and stood from the couch. "Say less," he agreed before heading out of the front door.

"Listen, Cuz. You gotta relax, my nigga. You can't think and be mad at the same time. I know that shit bothering you about what happened with DJ, but you can't find out shit if you moving like this. You'll be locked by morning at this rate, fool," Torey tried to calm his nerves.

Ryan took a seat next to him on the couch and exhaled a sigh of sadness. He was clutching on his Glock 40 tightly. "DJ was my fucking dawg. That's my best friend. How the fuck do you expect me to act?"

"That's understood. All I'm saying is that we ain't gonna be able to find out shit if you snapping and running everybody off. Now from what I'm hearing, this nigga Wicked supposed to have got out like yesterday or some shit like that. I didn't wanna just spill that shit on you right after you been grieving about bro because it might not be facts, but he might have had something to do with it."

"Wicked?" Ryan smacked his teeth as if that was an insult. "That nigga a whole pussy. He ain't even built like that to play with us. We been beating this nigga's ass since middle school, Torey."

"And what the fuck is that supposed to mean, Ryan? Just because you feel like you busted the nigga's head doesn't mean that a nigga can't turn into a beast overnight. You know it's not too many niggas lasting in that county, and he just did nearly seven months in that bitch. All I'm saying is you can't just sleep on anybody. That's how a nigga get they ass popped." Torey shrugged.

Ryan evaluated his words and had to take them into consideration, because anybody could lose their life at any moment. It was hard to gather around preparing for a funeral of a nigga so close to him, but he also thought about the niggas' lives he took in the boundaries of Wilmington. His cousin's words were more than correct. They were precise.

"Still and all, DJ didn't hang with too many niggas. Ain't nobody just pushing up on these two in Delaware."

"Ryan just had the press on all these fake-ass killas," Demerea added her input.

"What the fuck does that have to do with anything? You act like it's just one side of Delaware, and it damn sho' ain't just one killer." Torey ignored her dumb-ass comment.

"So what you saying?" Ryan asked, trying to stop all the fucking riddles.

"I'm saying that it could've been anyone you've had smoke with in the past six months. Ryan, I'm on the east side, and niggas all around my way stressing how bad they hate you. That's not including the west or the south. You've tarnished your name around this bitch, cut niggas out on making money, and stopping all the plugs' pockets from getting fat. This is the time to be cautious and limit who the fuck comes around. You moving weight, not kibbles, nigga. Somebody gotta move better." Torey shook his head.

His older cousin was right, and Ryan literally didn't have anything to say in his defense. The open movement of his operation was too exposed, and that shit was about to come to an end. "Fuck it. If it ain't you, I don't want nobody knowing where we conduct our business at from now on. I'm cutting back on all the extra workers and shortening down to whoever you feel we need. Me and Demerea about to trash this spot and relocate a little further into Philly where our whereabouts can't be as easily located. It's just family from now on. I'll let you explain it to Freddie. We can cut him a check and just send him on about his way until we get a whole new crew," Ryan ordered before standing to his feet.

"Now that sounds like a better plan to me. Where are you thinking about moving the spot to?" Torey asked.

"Probably down on Meek's block. Even though it's hot, none of them cats know us, and ain't nobody coming through them niggas trimming around. It's time to duck off and set the record straight with this shit. I only got a few more months of this hustling left in me, and then it's over."

"If you ain't doing nothing to harm me, you know I'm with it, nigga. What else is family for?" Torey shook Ryan's hand before leaving out the front door.

Chris Green

Chapter 18
Severe and Teona
8:43 p.m.

Pulling behind the abandoned store parking lot, Severe and Teona spotted Detective Bradley standing next to his unmarked police cruiser and pulled directly next to him. After parking their rental, Severe stepped out and Teona followed directly behind him. Severe walked over to Bradley and stopped a few feet away from him.

"I called this meet-up to let you know what's going on. You know I been searching up and down for this dude, and we finally got something accomplished."

Detective Bradley looked at him with a dumb expression. "Negro, it's been two months. I asked you to handle this business how long ago? I even gave you the address to where we would be after the table meetings. What could you possibly have done to accomplish anything if you ain't telling me what I want to know, Severe, and why the fuck is she here?" He nodded towards Teona.

"That's what I'm trying to tell you, Bradley. She's been the one helping me track this fool down. I tried to follow this nigga after the meetings like you told me, and he's always got a team meeting up with him afterwards to throw me off track. I can't follow three cars at one time if this nigga switching them bitches like Houdini," he stressed.

"So what did you possibly accomplish? I'm dying to know, because right now, I'm still not getting my extra payments, and I'm damn sure still stuck with this punk-ass kid in the seat at our table. "

"I found his little friend. The one he sells work with. See, these niggas move around like night and day. It's his right-hand man. I killed his ass on the strength, just to show that fool we ain't playing. My next move is to just catch Ryan at his funeral and do his ass right after he leaves. He can't do nothing without his potna because he don't run with too many more. That'll slow him down until I catch up. Kill two birds with one stone," Severe said as if he just made the best play in history.

Detective Bradley took a deep breath before rubbing his temple. "Let me guess. That right hand man is Darius Miller. Right?"

Severe frowned upon hearing the name. "I don't know nothing 'bout no government, but I know DJ. His ass is dead, and now we only gotta worry about Ryan."

"You stupid fucking idiot! You killed a fucking Princeton college student. My captain is all over my ass about a damn case that wasn't supposed to even happen. You murdered an innocent kid thinking that you was winning. How fucking stupid could you be?" Detective Bradley barked.

Severe looked back at Teona, dumbfounded. "I didn't know he was a fucking college student. I was just trying to handle the business. What's the big deal? It's not like they know." He blew the statement off as if it meant nothing.

Smiling, Detective Bradley shook his head. "You know what? You're absolutely right. It doesn't matter." Pulling a .45 automatic handgun from his shoulder holster, he shot Teona directly between the eyes. The blood from her brains splattered on Severe's shirt before he could even close his eyes.

"What the fuck?" Severe trembled in fear before looking down at her dead body. "What the hell is wrong with you, Bradley?" Severe sniffled, ready to shed a tear for the dead free pussy he would never touch again.

"You killed her, idiot. Not me. I asked you to do one thing: handle Ryan. Now you have the Feds crawling down my boss's throat, which places pressure on me. So the job will have to be completed without you."

"Wait!" Severe held up his hands. "I'll kill Ryan for free, Bradley. You ain't gotta do it like this for me since I screwed up. One more shot is all I need." He shook uncontrollably with a line of sweat rolling down his forehead.

"Cool. I'll give you one more shot," Detective Bradley agreed before placing a slug into the top of his head.

Wiping his fingerprints off the throwaway gun, he placed it into Severe's palm and walked back to his car. He cranked up the ignition and smashed off

* * *

Ryan and Demerea
1:14 a.m.

As he jumped up from his sleep, Ryan jerked his head violently, looking around the room.

Demerea sat up next to him and shook her head. "Was it another bad dream?"

Ryan's chest heaved with fear and sweat was pouring down his body like somebody had dumped a boiling pot of coffee over his face. "Yeah," he replied before sitting on the edge of the bed.

"You know what that is, Ryan. It's just your thoughts eating at you. Reckless was your friend, regardless of how you tried to look at it. Everybody really feels like you didn't do that," she admitted.

Ryan thought about the recent news he'd gotten earlier about Nas and Wicked. He knew that shit was beyond real. Freddie eventually pulled over to his crib after leaving Ryan's spot and made the call that shit was past bad. Before Ryan could ask, Freddie sent a video of the police flooded around Nas's crib. The realization of how close death was approaching really started to sink in.

Climbing out of the small bed, Ryan looked down at her. "Fuck three months. After this mission with me and Ghost gets handled, I'm walking away with you and my mama. I'm going to get Prince, even if I gotta take him myself. "

"You know I'll stand behind you no matter what, Ryan, but you gotta remain calm. You've been clutching on that gun in your sleep, and I don't want you to end up hurting me by accident." Demerea gave him a look of worry.

Nodding, Ryan placed the gun on his hip and grabbed the small joint out of the ashtray. He walked out of the hotel room. He stood on the balcony and let the cold air bring him back to reality. After all the things Delaware had to offer, Ryan never thought that he would be in the spot he was at the time. Half of his friends were gone, and the game he thought was good turned out to be the worst decision he ever made in his life. Nothing would ever be the same. Precious, DJ, Wicked, Reckless...even Nas. The numbers continued to add up, and death was ready to knock on Ryan's front door. It was only a matter of time if he didn't switch shit up.

Using his phone, he scrolled through the call log until he reached Kimyetta's phone number. Pressing the dial button, he waited patiently for an answer. After six rings, he was about to hang up, but her voice came through the line in a groggy tone.

"Ryan?"

"Hey Mama," he said as if it were his first day of school.

"Boy, it's damn near two in the morning. What do you want?"

"I was thinking about you, and just wanted to hear your voice," he lied.

"Yeah, right. Them demons haunting yo' ass, ain't it?" She sat up in her bed.

Ryan paused, wondering if she was able to read his mind. "How did you know?"

"Because, dumbass, yo' daddy used to wake me out of my damn sleep around the same time doing the same shit. I warned you, Ryan. Yo' hard-headed ass don't listen."

"I'm really messed up, Ma. I don't know what else to do. DJ was the closest friend I had."

"And you lost him to the same streets that you're not trying to give up on, Ryan. Think about what you're saying. DJ was your friend and you watched him lose his life a day before going to college. What in the hell do you think can happen to you? This isn't *Wheel of Fortune* so I don't expect you to guess anything either, boy. These are things you should already know," Kimyetta huffed.

"It's not that."

"Then what is it, Ryan?"

It wasn't like he could just say that he was waiting for a moment to meet the plug so his out of state homeboy could murder her. That was some shit she would never understand. The life of being at a round table where your soul being taken depended on if a coin was missing from your payments... It wasn't easy to just walk away. "I'm really trying to wrap this up. I don't wanna hustle anymore, and I don't wanna die, Ma. It's just a lot of things that you wouldn't understand."

Shuffling in her covers. Kimyetta sat on the edge of her bed. "Listen, Ryan. For twenty years I stayed with your father and watched him suffer through these nasty-ass streets. He didn't wanna quit, no matter how much he lied or tried to calm my nerves saying that he would. Your dad thought that shit didn't stink, Ryan. He killed, he hustled, and even crossed out the ones he loved for being a part of this shit y'all call the game. That shit caused him to leave first with the possibility of never coming home. After that, he lost himself. Your father tried to cheat life and lost with death because there is no winning, Ryan. You can't win. That's the trick to it, son. Get yourself together before it's too late, because I will not be burying you. I promise." She hung up in his ear.

Placing the phone back into his pocket, Ryan lit the small joint in his hand and exhaled the cloud of smoke into the air. Every word she said was more than real, but the reality of life and death was past coming. It was right at his doorstep. There was only one chance to straighten the devil from his path, and that was a chance he anticipated to come very soon.

Chapter 19
One month later
11:44 p.m.
Midnight Cartel meeting

Ryan drove into the parking lot of the bar. He parked his car and collected the large bag of cash from the backseat. It was the same thing as always. The driveway was nearly dry, which obviously meant that it wasn't much movement inside the establishment. After finishing the last of his blunt, he put the roach out inside the ashtray hole. Stepping out of his new white 2019 Tahoe, he opened the trunk and grabbed the two small duffle bags full of cash. While making his way towards the building, he spotted the same usual dickheads standing out front.

Unlike the other nights of them letting him slide through, one of the guards placed his hand on Ryan's chest. "Pat search," he said aggressively.

"Pat search? Motherfucker, I been working here for the past six months. I ain't been getting patted down, nigga." Ryan set down the bags and placed his hands on the wall.

"I don't give a fuck if you were a thirty year vet. Tonight is different." He returned Ryan's aggression as the other guard continued to stand post. He ran his hand past the pistol on Ryan's hip. He removed it and placed it in his lower back. "You'll receive it back once you're done."

"Yeah, whateva, muthafucka," Ryan mumbled before picking up the bags to head inside.

As he stepped through the door, the empty dance floor instantly made him paranoid. The jukebox was crooning a slow country tune and Lizzy was standing behind the bar sipping on a Long Island iced tea. Ryan moved over to her with a curious expression plastered on his face.

"Hey honey bun." She smiled before sipping her drink again. "They're already downstairs waiting. You might wanna make your way on down 'cause things seem to be kinda important tonight," she whispered with a country drawl.

"Where the hell is everyone? Why is the bar so empty?" Ryan looked around at all the empty space.

"Richard requested a closed session tonight. It beats me. I'm not getting paid to ask questions. I only follow orders, honey bun. They're waiting for you." Lizzy nodded towards the door that led to the basement floor.

Ryan shrugged his shoulders and continued to his destination. After stepping through the door, he began to wonder if Richard had anything slick up his sleeve. It had been six months of cashing in every two weeks. The payments were always in full, and the thought of what Lucci Bruno warned him about began to run through his mind.

"After they're done with you, and you make a few runs perfectly, they get rid of you." It was the only way the table worked according to the way he explained a few months back.

When Ryan got down to the bottom of the steps, he saw that the buff bodyguard who usually stood on the inside until he heard a knock was now posted outside like an on-duty cop. His face happened to soften when he spotted Ryan. He gave him a head nod without all the hostility that he usually carried. He opened the door, allowing Ryan to walk directly inside. Ryan was now thinking about the gun the bodyguard removed from his hip upstairs. If a nigga was to get into a full-blown shootout, he knew that his chances of getting away were zero to none.

Ryan walked around the corner and spotted Richard sitting at the table with the few members that were still a part of the cartel.

"Ryan. Welcome, my friend." Richard grinned like the main introduction was about to start or some shit.

Instead of replying, Ryan set the bags by Summer and Winter's feet and took his seat. The two women grabbed a bag apiece and made their way inside the office, closing the door behind them. Richard continued to sit for a second and happened to glance at his watch. After seeing that it was one minute before midnight, he rose to his feet and clasped his hands.

"Welcome to the Midnight Cartel. I would like to take the time to introduce a major problem that was holding us back. I mean a big problem as a whole. Detective Christopher Bradley. The one who introduced us to this all-star Ryan here. Unfortunately, it seems that he pulled a hideous stunt that placed us in the fucking spotlight of all the big authorities, and that is just a shame. Let's give him a chance to speak for himself." Richard pointed over to Ryan. "If you don't mind, could you slide his chair out a little more please? He's probably suffocating inside of there."

Ryan looked down two seats from him and spotted a black garbage bag sitting inside the chair. He was about to respond until he spotted the blood that was leaking out of it onto the floor. Looking closer, he noticed the Delaware police badge hanging from the bottom and nearly puked.

"Well, I guess Ryan doesn't want anything to do with Bradley either, huh?" Richard slapped his thigh before cracking up with laughter. He smoothed his silky hair back and exhaled heavily. "To my knowledge, Detective Bradley killed two people that were outside the bounds of this business. We run a fucking operation, people, and if you're not ordered to do anything from me, that means it's not fucking allowed!" he shouted loudly with a vein protruding from the center of his forehead.

Ryan's heartbeat increased when he cut his eyes quickly over to him before finishing what he had to say.

"The funny thing is, he was doing this because of your sloppiness, Ryan. I've heard that you've been very interactive with people. A lot of fucking people, Ryan. When we allowed you to step inside of this business, I explained that the rules were to move alone. That means no friends. No family should have had ties with you about the supply of this cartel. You obviously disobeyed, from what Summer and Winter tell me. I've watched you, Ryan. We followed you. We've monitored your movements, and I have to say that you've disappointed me with those actions. Still and all, you're a great team player, which is the only reason we've never removed you from this spot. Do you have anything to say for yourself?" Richard crossed one leg over the other before looking at the time. The other three table members looked at him with sealed lips as if they were waiting for an answer also.

Ryan truly didn't know what to say, because obviously his death would be approaching after whatever he decided to reply with. He looked Richard in his eyes and told the truth. "I did what I had to in order for the product to get pushed. As far as anyone knowing about the status of this table, that has never happened. Detective Bradley was responsible for killing my associate, and now that just leaves me to handle this alone. I can't make any excuses." He sat back in his seat, awaiting the bullet that was bound to come next.

Before Richard could reply, he caught sight of a middle-aged Spanish woman stepping out of the small office room. Ryan's eyes locked on to her immediately as she sashayed with a powerful strut over to stand behind Richard. Her hair was wrapped in a bun, and a white Saint Laurent dress was tailored on her body to perfection. Her smile alone spelled authority, and that's when he realized who was standing in front of him.

Richard turned around and kissed the back of her hand as if she was the Goddess of Greece. "Eva, I would like you to meet the last of our table, and the one who's been our superstar with making his business number one. Ryan." Richard looked over to him with a nervous expression.

Ryan was too busy sliding the cell phone out of his pocket, pressing the number to speed dial Ghost's number. He set it on his lap and flashed Eva the most handsome smile possible. "It's a great pleasure to meet you, boss lady."

Her evil eyes spelled out the terror that she could cause, and from the looks of all the expensive jewelry on her body, she was bigger than just Delaware. "Hello, Ryan. I've heard that you've made me a lot of money. That's good, for your sake," Eva stated dryly before looking back down at Richard. "You have twenty minutes left. From the looks of things, we need more workers. I would suggest that you use this star player of yours to find some. I'm only here to remind you guys to keep up the good work. I don't like being upset, but lately this portion of my table has made me very happy with your work ethics. Remember to never lose that, because if you do, that means Richard will lose himself, and you will too." She rubbed Richard's shoulder as if he was just a pet.

The phone call with Ghost was now ended, giving Ryan the indication that he got the signal just like he asked. Eva's eyes roamed over Ryan as if she was studying him. "It was nice meeting you, Mr. All-star. The rest of you have also met the requirements to be a part of this lucrative group. Be careful with any future movements. You wouldn't want them to be your last." Eva patted Richard's shoulder and headed back inside the small office, closing the door behind her.

Turning to face the table, Richard cleared his throat. "As I said before the boss lady walked in, I would like to take this chance to clear the air on what's about to occur. Ryan, for your stupidity and outrageous movements, your supply has been boosted to sixty keys every two weeks."

"What? Richard, that's impossible. I can't sell sixty keys in two weeks. I barely could top the forty that you were dishing on me." Ryan sat up with an angry face.

"Hey, kid. Boss lady's orders. I could give a fuck about what you feel. If you haven't got it through your head yet, no one talks back, Ryan. This isn't an option. It's an order." He pulled a handgun from his suit jacket and placed it on the table.

"I can handle it," a voice said from a short distance away.

Ryan turned his head to see Ghost standing at the entrance with a silenced assault rifle in his hands. "Go ahead and reach for it, Lieutenant Richard. Your head will be gone before you can blink, bitch." His voice was low enough to where only the individuals in the room could hear him.

Ghost closed their distance quickly and snatched the pistol sliding it on his hip. "Where is she?"

Richard sat back in his seat with a smile. "Chance Grey. Is that you?"

"I'll ask you one last time." Ghost placed the barrel to his head.

Richard's lips trembled, and he could feel the pit of his stomach bubbling. "Fuck you, Ghost. You still won't win," he mumbled under his breath before closing his eyes.

"Incorrect," Ghost replied before placing a slug through his forehead. The bullet was silent as a whistle, and Richard's head splattered across the cartel meeting table. Turning the gun towards the members, Ghost began to gun them all down one by one.

Toot! Toot! Toot! Toot! Toot! Toot!

Aiming the gun at Ryan, he flashed him a crooked smile. "Where is she?" he whispered.

Ryan pointed at the small office door that sat fifteen feet away from them.

"Leave now." Ghost nodded towards the exit.

Ryan was shaking like a leaf from how fast the entire room had been placed to sleep. Standing from the table, he slowly moved past him and took flight out of the small exit door. The bulky bodyguard rested outside with a bullet between his eyes. Trying to block the images from his mind, Ryan stepped over him, and made his way quickly up the stairs.

Ghost aimed his gun with expertise at the office door. Moving forward, he slammed his foot into it, causing that bitch to crash down.

* * *

Chris Green

8:35 a. m.
Faith's trial, Delaware Superior Courthouse

The trial for Faith was now in effect, and the district attorney started off early in the courtroom with blasting her name horribly. Within thirty minutes of the court hearing, Mr. Robinson flapped his mouth with unconstitutional statements, which was accepted by the slow judge sitting in front of them. His evidence was on the floor, and not one witness was able to step up in the presence of Faith and point her out. Black Girl's mother had produced the other funds for Mr. Jeff Hovecek to take the case. His attitude was very aggressive, and he assured Faith his game plan would work. Shit wasn't gonna go how the district attorney thought. It was hard to follow his lead with being quiet, especially when Mr. Robinson continued to bash her name for killing Precious. Still, remembering that she was in trial, Faith held her composure and watched as the man ranted.

"Now the State will rest, Judge Crump, but I ask you to please look at this case with your experienced eyes. This girl is a cold-blooded murderer of this poor innocent college student, and she needs to be brought to justice," he stated before sitting back down in his seat.

Judge Crump nodded and slid his attention over to Jeff Hovecek who sat as if he didn't have a care in the world. "Attorney Hovecek, do you have anything else before we close out, sir?"

Faith didn't know what he had planned, but it was the closing arguments, and her heart was beating like a nigga mashed a twelve inch penis into her tummy. She watched him get up and pop his collar like he had that shit in the bag. "Yes I would, Your Honor. I would like to point out

162

three things before closing." He waved for the detective to bring forth the decoy weapon. "This is a .380 automatic pistol, a gun similar to the one that murdered this young lady. I would like the jury to understand that in life, a lot of things aren't about the eloquent words that you can spill out of your mouth to take someone's freedom. It's about the evidence."

Jeff Hovecek grabbed the gun from the detective's hands and placed it on the table in front of Faith. She looked up at him confused, but his confident smirk confirmed that he was sure of what needed to be done. Jeff stepped to the front of the courtroom where he could look out at all the people who crowded the room.

"Faith Anderson, do you know what type of gun that is sitting in front of you right now? Please speak into the microphone so we can hear you clearly, please. "

"Yes." Her voice echoed through the courtroom.

"Good. Tell us what type of gun it is," he replied.

Faith huffed lightly and looked down at the engagements on the side. "It's a .380 snapshot handgun," she answered.

"Correct. Faith, have you ever shot a gun in your life?

"Yes."

"On how many occasions?" Jeff Hovecek walked around in a slow pace without looking at her.

Faith didn't know what the hell that had to do with anything, but she still complied with his question. "Numerous times. My dad is an army veteran so I've been trained on how to shoot since I was child."

"Okay. Faith, if you don't mind, I would like you to pick up the gun and hold it in your hand please. Picture you and your dad training. That's what I want you to picture. It's not loaded. Go ahead," Jeff encouraged as the courtroom sat in silence.

Faith looked around nervously but still obliged. Picking it up with her right hand, she held it as if she was hunting.

"Good, now can you place it back down please?" her lawyer ordered politely.

Faith followed his rules, setting it down.

"Ms. Anderson, can you please pick up the weapon again please?" Jeff Hovecek looked at her sternly.

Faith stared at him with a crazy face, but picked the gun up again with her right hand and held it out.

"Thank you, Ms. Anderson. Please set it back down."

This process occurred twice before Jeff Hovecek turned around and faced Judge Crump and the jury. "Now we've seen Ms. Anderson in action with the way that she's used to handling a gun. Let's take a look at my second witness's testimony." Placing the small DVD video into the small projector, he turned it on, and pointed towards the clerk to dim the lights. Once the video began, you could see the image of a woman from a distance walking towards Precious's vehicle as she dug inside the backseat. The film was clear. Everyone watched as Precious fumbled to climb out of her car. The woman who held the gun in her left hand fired instantly once Precious was able to turn around and spot her attacker. Her body crashed to the ground, and the woman ran off slowly until the video wasn't able to catch vision of her anymore.

"Now I will rewind this video again so you all can see this clearly one last time," Jeff Hovecek said, pressing the button on the projector

Faith couldn't help but to watch the video closer. The sight of the woman who held the gun stood out to her like a sore thumb. It was like looking into a reflecting mirror. She just couldn't be sure because her face was covered. The shakiness in her hands when the gun fired clarified it all. When the woman turned around to run, Faith's eyes grew wide in shock. Even a mask couldn't hide her identity.

The lights came back on and Jeff Hovecek looked around the courtroom. "Your Honor, from the video, you can clearly see that the woman who was shooting the gun isn't Faith for three reasons. First, Faith has been dealing with weapons her entire life, since she was a child. Her father is an army veteran. The woman in the video is clearly not capable of handling the weapon because she's unstable with this weapon that's in her hands. Secondly, I asked Ms. Anderson to pick up the weapon that was similar to the weapon in the video numerous times. She picked the gun up over six times," Jeff Hovecek said with confidence.

Judge Crump looked at him as if it didn't make sense. "You still have to be direct, Mr. Hovecek."

"Faith grabbed the gun and aimed it numerous times with her right hand. The woman who was in the video used the gun in her left hand the entire time, even when she fired. As an experienced pistol user like myself, I asked her to pick up the weapon numerous times, and off instincts and being right-handed, that's the hand she used. It is quite common for anyone who's a gun owner, Your Honor. That alone clears my client."

Faith had to admit that he was on the roll. From the look of the jury who were nodding their heads, he had the case wrapped up.

Jeff Hovecek stepped up to the stand and pointed at a woman who was sitting in the crowd of the citizens and asked her to stand. "Your Honor, my last proof is this prudent woman right here. I'll allow her to introduce herself," he said before allowing the Spanish-looking chick to speak.

The district attorney, Mr. Robinson, looked back at her with hatred, wondering what trick was up Jeff Hovecek's sleeve.

"Your Honor, my name is Vivian Hullo. I'm a forensics investigator and analyst. When I got the call from Jeff Hovecek about this incident, I instantly dug into it in order to see whether this case could be solved or if I could help. During my investigation, I followed certain procedures and steps to determine whether she matched the suspect, and it still came up inconclusive." The woman pushed her glasses up in a nerdy motion.

Judge Crump leaned forward in his chair. "Is there any way you can break that description down into English for me?" He was scratching the side of his head.

Ms. Hullo shrugged. "I investigate size, height, and other details of videos that involve murders. I have all the necessary equipment to see if anybody matches the description if their face is not able to be seen. The woman in the video isn't Ms. Anderson. She's too tall. Faith is 4'9". Whoever that is on there is over 5'7". I'm an expert, and I've done this over fourteen years, sir." She nodded with assurance before sitting back down.

"Objection, Your Honor. We can't sit here and listen to testimony from this woman that was brought into the courts on a blind eye. The proper procedure is to have them all present before trial. This is the end of our case, so any other testimonies will have to be excluded from what we've already discovered today in this courtroom, sir."

The District attorney frowned at the action Faith's lawyer was trying to pull.

Sighing, Judge Crump rubbed his temple. "As a superior state official of the law, I'm inclined to agree. The time for witnesses has been slashed at this moment, so I'll ask both sides: are the closing arguments finished so I can make a decision on this? I'm not going to be able to accept this woman's statement." He motioned for the forensics investigator to take a seat.

After getting Faith's lawyer's approval to proceed without his last trick up the sleeve, Judge Crump glanced back to the arrogant D.A.

"Yes, Your Honor. We just would like to let the jury know that even though the family isn't here present at tria, they still deserve justice for this horrendous crime. Faith Anderson deserves to spend the rest of her life in jail and should not be released back on the streets. That'll be all. The state will rest." He bit down on his jaw, slightly angry from how the end of his argument got destroyed.

"Well in that case, we can let the jury deliberate. Should we call a small recess?" Judge Crump asked Jeff Hovecek.

"No sir. Me and my client will wait right here until this is settled. I have a feeling that it's not going to take long at all."

After the jury left, the silence around the courtroom fell as if the people were waiting to bury a close relative. The theory of what Jeff Hovecek said was definitely true, because not even twenty-five minutes after the jury left. They were piling back into their spaces on the bench. All of their heads turned to look at Faith. The action caused her stomach to turn, but even after that, she didn't fold.

Once Judge Crump made his way back to the power seat. He looked over to the speaker for the jury board, and nodded. A frail white woman rose to her feet and glanced down at a small piece of paper in her hand. "We the jury find Faith Anderson on the count of Murder One...not guilty."

Faith's head fell into her hands and the tears couldn't help but to fall after hearing those strong words.

Jeff Hovecek patted her back before whispering into her ear. "Raise your head. Show them who won."

Lifting her head with a smile, Faith leaped up,] and wrapped him into a giant hug. "Thank you so much, Mr. Hovecek. I owe you big time for this," Faith said with excitement in her tone.

"No need. Black Girl's mother supported me more than you can imagine. I'll have you released by morning," he guaranteed, flashing her a big smile.

"Well. The court has made a decision, Mr. Robinson. This case is final. You may take Ms. Anderson back to the jail where she can be processed out," Judge Crump ordered before banging his gavel.

The depression on District Attorney Robinson's face increased as he watched Jeff Hovecek shake hands with the judge. The two bailiffs in the courtroom escorted Faith back towards the holding tanks, and all she could think about was the way her freedom had just been granted.

It was more than a blessing. It felt great to get her justification from the misidentification. Now the business was more personal. All she could think about was her next plan: making everyone who crossed her pay. Forcing them to see that they all made a grave mistake was pumping through her mind. She wanted more than just revenge. She wanted power.

Chris Green

Chapter 20

When she got back to the prison, Faith entered her cell, causing Black Girl to rise up on her bed. Judging from the sight of her face she could tell that things didn't go as planned.

"What happened?" Black Girl asked with her heart thumping in fear of the worst.

"The same thing that always happens for an innocent bitch like me," Faith said before a large smile widened across her cheeks.

Jumping up, Black Girl grabbed her, squeezing tightly. "I told you. I told you. Oh my God! I'm so happy for you, Faith. You did it," she stressed, nearly in tears.

The truth was so crazy because Faith felt that she was placed around Black Girl for a reason. She was really a true blessing. "No, girl. I couldn't have done this without you. I've never had anyone help me through something so deep. I owe you more than everything." She wiped the tears from her own eyes.

"That's what friends are for. You know you my li'l widow. I gotta write down all my information for you," Black Girl said before grabbing a pen and sitting on her bed. "And don't be acting brand new when you step into that free world. You know how y'all chicken heads act when y'all leave a bitch in here. I want letters and pictures every week." She laughed.

"Girl, I'm not worried about nobody but you. I need visitation rights and everything. It's a whole new start for me so I'm moving right, and you ain't never gotta worry about shit while I'm out there. That's a promise," Faith assured her.

"Well, I know one thing. I'ma be ready. I'm so happy for you." Black Girl stood up to grab her small phone book out of the locker box.

Faith's eyes roamed her body up and down and smiled. "Thank you, girl. You mean too much in my heart, especially for what you did with my lawyer. Besides, it's my turn anyway."

"What do you mean? Your turn for what?" she replied with a confused expression.

Faith slapped Black Girl's giant booty, making it jiggle like Jell-O. She closed the small distance between them. "To take that sweet shit right there. Now pull them pants off and bend yo' ass over." Faith bit on her bottom lip seductively.

Black girl snickered. "Really? So you just gonna take it, huh, Faith?"

"You still talking. Take them pants off and bend that good shit over before I beat that ass." Faith folded her arms with a smile. "And my name is the Black Widow. Remember that."

"Damn, okay my little Widow." Black Girl's pussy slightly tingled from Faith's freaky ass attitude. Pulling her sweats down, she shook her beautiful round ass, forcing it to move like a wave.

Staring at her gorgeous body and skin, Faith licked her lips and quickly covered the window of their cell.

* * *

Ryan's new spot, 8:47 p.m.

Walking through the door of his cousin's home, Torey looked over at Demerea's fat belly self whipping in the kitchen and took a seat on the couch.

"Hey Torey. You want something to eat while I'm up on my feet?" she asked while making herself a small bowl of her masterpiece.

"Nah. I'm waiting for Ryan's ass to get back out this damn shower so I can see whether he wants me to grab that extra supply out of his trunk. I ain't got long either," he replied while glancing at his watch.

"Cool, whatever floats ya boat," she said before heading back to her bedroom.

Looking around the nice three-bedroom crib, Torey sat back and relaxed on the couch. It had been a long day, and he was in desperate need of some ass from a quick thot. Ryan's phone ringing on the living room table caught his attention. Grabbing it, he looked at the name on the front and forwarded it to the voicemail. He looked at the whack-ass picture of Ryan posted on the front. He cracked a small laugh. "Fake-ass DMX wannabe," he mumbled to himself.

Pressing the gallery button, he began to scroll through his pictures. The ones of DJ caused him to smile. He knew that the two of them were true friends. It was ugly how the game got played, but unfortunately, not everyone was allowed to make it. Scrolling down further, his heart slightly stopped when he spotted the picture of Ryan sitting in the club. His cousin wasn't relevant, but the nigga sitting in the background was. Turning the brightness on the screen up, he stared at the man closer and he knew that his mind wasn't playing tricks on him. Digging in his pocket, he pulled out his wallet, and removed the picture of his father Antwan. Looking up to be sure that Demerea wasn't coming back out of the room, he held up the picture and looked back and forth between his dad and the man who resembled him on

Ryan's phone. They were an exact replica, as if he had placed them on a printer machine.

That's when Ryan's comment from a while back crept into his head. *"Nah, his name is Ghost, you don't know him. He's an older nigga from Atlanta."* Torey replayed it back through his head as he stared at the picture of Ghost, screenshotting the picture. He forwarded it to his phone and then placed it back on Ryan's coffee table. He was so distraught at the moment that he couldn't even sit in his home anymore. The supply, the money, none of that shit mattered anymore. It was clear what was taking place, and now shit was about to get exposed. Standing to his feet, he left Ryan's home without alerting him or Demerea.

Chapter 21
9:45 a.m.
The next morning

Demerea laid in the hospital bed, panting heavily as the sweat rolled down her forehead. Ryan stood next to her with a big smile on his face. It took fifteen long, hard minutes, but the healthy baby was finally here. After waking up late during the night, Demerea's water broke a month early, and their little bundle of joy was ready to make her way into the world. After struggling to get to the hospital, Ryan watched his beautiful baby girl Breanna be birthed into the world, seven pounds and two ounces. She was his exact replica.

"Mama, here is your little one," the female doctor said as she placed Breanna into Demerea's arms.

"Oh my Godddd!" She smiled. "She looks just like you, Daddy!" She snickered, looking up into Ryan's face.

"She looks like us," he chimed in with excitement.

For the next thirty minutes they sat and watched as their little one breathed lightly in her mother's grasp.

"So do you think that I made you happy enough with this beautiful little girl? You asked for a family, nigga." Demerea smirked arrogantly.

Ryan couldn't help but laugh. "Of course I'm happy. This is about to be a new start. You just better make sure you mind your manners, and make sure you let these niggas out here know that shit on lock," he checked her ass back.

His attention was broken when the hospital door opened up. Ryan looked up into Faith's eyes, and literally felt his heart drop. Her hair was pulled to the back in a long ponytail. A Gucci shirt was fitted around her perfect breasts. A pair of black Gucci jeans matched the sneakers on her feet, and the black mascara on her eyes made her seem as if she had gotten older, but sexier. She was on her true grown woman shit. "Faith?" he said in shock.

Demerea couldn't help but to force a bright smile. "You're really home," she said sarcastically.

"Yeah. I am," Faith said with her hands positioned behind her calmly as if she was waiting for an explanation.

"How did you find us?" Ryan asked suspiciously with nervousness lacing his tone.

"That doesn't matter, Ryan," Demerea butted in. "Faith, I would like you to meet me and Ryan's beautiful baby girl Breanna." She smiled with a devilish grin.

Faith smiled lightly. "It's good to meet you, Breanna," she said coldly before removing the 9mm pistol from behind her back, aiming it at Demerea's head. She pulled the trigger before she could blink.

The slug caused her body to lock up, forcing the baby to clench in Demerea's arms tightly. Her loud screams erupted at the feeling of her mother's dead body easing back on the pillow.

"Faithhhh, nooo!" Ryan screamed like a pure bitch. The medical staff outside of the doors had started to scramble once the gunshot sounded off.

"You truly fucked up, Ryan. You deceived me, you left me for dead, and you pulled the slimiest shit that you could against me. I could kill you right now, but I have a lot of other plans to complete before that."

Ryan stood with his mouth wide open as his baby continued to yell at the top of her lungs. "Faith!" He held up his hands knowing that his gun wasn't near him.

"The name isn't Faith. It's Black Widow. Grab your child and leave. I'll see you again, Ryan. Go ahead." She smiled wickedly while waving the gun at him.

Reaching down for Breanna, Ryan grabbed her and slowly made his way to the door. Faith moved around the room as he edged his way to the door. Once he got close enough, he cuffed his child and ran out.

Faith couldn't help but look over at Demerea's body and laugh. Aiming the weapon at her again, she released six more slugs into her body

Boom! Boom! Boom! Boom! Boom! Boom!

"Congratulations, bitch." Faith smiled before walking out of the room, leaving her havoc behind.

* * *

Twenty-five minutes later

After pulling up in front of his home, Ryan quickly rushed inside and grabbed all of his stash that was hidden under his kitchen cabinet. His hands were shaking horribly as he tried to grab all the necessary things he needed.

He ran to grab a few of his guns from under the mattress. He headed back out of the front door and jumped in the car. The sight of his little daughter wrapped in the blanket and car seat calmed him before he put the car in drive and sped off.

Ryan was moving so fast that he never paid attention to the whip sitting across the street. Once his car gained a small distance away from the house, the black vehicle slowly pulled off behind him.

* * *

The drive to Kimyetta's house took over one hour. Pulling down in front of her two-bedroom home, Ryan grabbed the baby and stepped out. He was sure to leave the guns in the car so that Kimyetta wouldn't get paranoid. He didn't need her to flip before he could even explain what was at hand.

He walked up to the front door and knocked, and she answered within seconds. Flashing him a suspicious look, she pulled him inside and shut the door. Ryan moved slowly over to the couch, and took a seat.

"What the fuck is going on, Ryan? I've been looking at the news and I heard that it was a shooting at Demerea's hospital. Why are you here with that baby?" she questioned with her arms folded. Her foot was tapping against the floor rapidly.

"Mama. It happened so fast that I couldn't even move." Ryan set the baby down with ease before clasping his hands together.

"What happened, Ryan?" She was nearly in tears knowing what he was about to say.

"Demerea's dead." He lowered his head.

Kimyetta placed a hand over her mouth in shock. Before she could reply, her front door was opened, and Torey stepped through with his gun aimed directly for her.

Kimyetta's eyes widened in fear, but the bullet he placed between her eyes silenced any words that were about to come from her mouth.

Ryan raised his head just as she dropped to the floor.

"Mammmaaa!" he yelled, crawling to the ground.

Gazing up at Torey, he tried to speak, but fumbled over his words before getting them out. "Torey? What the fuck, man? What the fuck, Torey?"

"Quiet down, bitch nigga," he replied calmly.

"Bro, you just killed my mama, Torey. What the fuck did I do to you? God, please no! Mama, please!" Ryan cried, feeling as if the world was crashing down upon him.

"I'll tell you, Cousin. First off, you lied, and quite frankly, I hate liars, nigga."

"Torey, I've never lied to you about shit. Nothing! I was feeding you, nigga!" Ryan bit his bottom lip as snot poured from his nostrils. His eyes were turning bloodshot red, and it was now the second time he regretted not holding the pistol on him.

"Oh, you've lied more than once. See, I stood behind you. I worked for you, and helped push this little punk-ass weight. But I asked you about your little friend, and you said that I didn't know him. Turns out, I know him better than you do, motherfucker!" Torey said with a psychotic laugh.

"What the fuck are you talking about, man?

"Ghost."

"Torey, Ghost is gone. He's nobody that I even really know. I only did business with him. That shit has been over. What does this have to do with me?"

Torey huffed and decided to fill him in. "See, you move sloppy, Ryan, and I asked you not to place me in anything if it would harm me. Since I was a young kid, I've traveled from group home to group home. I eventually ended up in Delaware and landed inside of your wonderful family through adoption. Not only that, I happened to run from my history and past, thinking that it would leave, but out of all the little shit I couldn't forget, it was a nigga who was supposed to be my family killing my father and mother, taking them away from me, and leaving me to suffer in this cold world alone. After eighteen years of them being gone, I find this same man who took that away from me snapping pictures with my cousin in the club. Mr. Ghost himself."

"Torey, I don't know anything about this. You have to believe me. I'm your cousin," Ryan begged with his lips trembling.

Torey paused and looked him deeply in the eyes. "And he was my uncle," he said before placing a slug through Ryan's head. The bullet exited the back of his skull, causing his body to twitch as it collapsed on top of Kimyetta.

Looking around the small home, Torey huffed and took a deep breath. Digging in his pocket, he pulled his cell phone out, searched Google for the nearest airport, and placed the call. He listened to the phone ring.

A customer service representative answered, "Delta Airlines. This is Stewart. How may I help you?"

"Hi, Stewart. I would like to book a flight, please."

"Okay, sir. Where would you be booking this flight to?"

"Atlanta.

"Okay, sir. May I have your name please?"

Torey smiled evilly before walking out the front door. "Torey Ramirez."

To Be Continued...
Midnight Cartel 4
Coming Soon

180

Submission Guideline

Submit the first three chapters of your completed manuscript to ldpsubmissions@gmail.com, subject line: Your book's title. The manuscript must be in a .doc file and sent as an attachment. Document should be in Times New Roman, double spaced and in size 12 font. Also, provide your synopsis and full contact information. If sending multiple submissions, they must each be in a separate email.

Have a story but no way to send it electronically? You can still submit to LDP/Ca$h Presents. Send in the first three chapters, written or typed, of your completed manuscript to:

LDP: Submissions Dept
Po Box 944
Stockbridge, Ga 30281

DO NOT send original manuscript. Must be a duplicate.

Provide your synopsis and a cover letter containing your full contact information.

Thanks for considering LDP and Ca$h Presents.

Chris Green

By **Ghost**

A HUSTLER'S DECEIT III

KILL ZONE **II**

BAE BELONGS TO ME III

A DOPE BOY'S QUEEN III

By **Aryanna**

COKE KINGS V

KING OF THE TRAP II

By **T.J. Edwards**

GORILLAZ IN THE BAY V

3X KRAZY III

De'Kari

THE STREETS ARE CALLING II

Duquie Wilson

KINGPIN KILLAZ IV

STREET KINGS III

PAID IN BLOOD III

CARTEL KILLAZ IV

DOPE GODS III

Hood Rich

SINS OF A HUSTLA II

ASAD

KINGZ OF THE GAME VI

Playa Ray

SLAUGHTER GANG IV

RUTHLESS HEART IV

By Willie Slaughter

Chris Green

THE HEART OF A SAVAGE III
By Jibril Williams
FUK SHYT II
By Blakk Diamond
TRAP QUEEN
By Troublesome
YAYO V
GHOST MOB II
Stilloan Robinson
KINGPIN DREAMS III
By Paper Boi Rari
CREAM II
By Yolanda Moore
SON OF A DOPE FIEND III
By Renta
FOREVER GANGSTA II
GLOCKS ON SATIN SHEETS III
By Adrian Dulan
LOYALTY AIN'T PROMISED III
By Keith Williams
THE PRICE YOU PAY FOR LOVE II
By Destiny Skai
I'M NOTHING WITHOUT HIS LOVE II
SINS OF A THUG II
By Monet Dragun
LIFE OF A SAVAGE IV
MURDA SEASON IV

GANGLAND CARTEL III

CHI'RAQ GANGSTAS III

By **Romell Tukes**

QUIET MONEY IV

EXTENDED CLIP II

By **Trai'Quan**

THE STREETS MADE ME III

By **Larry D. Wright**

IF YOU CROSS ME ONCE II

ANGEL III

By **Anthony Fields**

FRIEND OR FOE III

By **Mimi**

SAVAGE STORMS III

By **Meesha**

BLOOD ON THE MONEY III

By J-Blunt

THE STREETS WILL NEVER CLOSE II

By K'ajji

NIGHTMARES OF A HUSTLA III

By King Dream

THE WIFEY I USED TO BE II

By Nicole Goosby

IN THE ARM OF HIS BOSS

By Jamila

MONEY, MURDER & MEMORIES II

Malik D. Rice

CONCRETE KILLAZ II
By Kingpen
HARD AND RUTHLESS II
By Von Wiley Hall
LEVELS TO THIS SHYT II
By Ah'Million
MOB TIES II
By SayNoMore

Available Now

RESTRAINING ORDER **I & II**
By **CA$H & Coffee**
LOVE KNOWS NO BOUNDARIES **I II & III**
By **Coffee**
RAISED AS A GOON I, II, III & IV
BRED BY THE SLUMS I, II, III
BLAST FOR ME I & II
ROTTEN TO THE CORE I II III
A BRONX TALE I, II, III
DUFFLE BAG CARTEL I II III IV V
HEARTLESS GOON I II III IV V
A SAVAGE DOPEBOY I II
DRUG LORDS I II III
CUTTHROAT MAFIA I II
By **Ghost**

LAY IT DOWN **I & II**

LAST OF A DYING BREED I II

BLOOD STAINS OF A SHOTTA I & II III

By **Jamaica**

LOYAL TO THE GAME I II III

LIFE OF SIN I, II III

By **TJ & Jelissa**

BLOODY COMMAS I & II

SKI MASK CARTEL I II & III

KING OF NEW YORK I II,III IV V

RISE TO POWER I II III

COKE KINGS I II III IV

BORN HEARTLESS I II III IV

KING OF THE TRAP

By **T.J. Edwards**

IF LOVING HIM IS WRONG…I & II

LOVE ME EVEN WHEN IT HURTS I II III

By **Jelissa**

WHEN THE STREETS CLAP BACK I & II III

THE HEART OF A SAVAGE I II

By **Jibril Williams**

A DISTINGUISHED THUG STOLE MY HEART I II & III

LOVE SHOULDN'T HURT I II III IV

RENEGADE BOYS I II III IV

PAID IN KARMA I II III

SAVAGE STORMS I II

By **Meesha**

Chris Green

A GANGSTER'S CODE I &, II III
A GANGSTER'S SYN I II III
THE SAVAGE LIFE I II III
CHAINED TO THE STREETS I II III
BLOOD ON THE MONEY I II
By J-Blunt
PUSH IT TO THE LIMIT
By **Bre' Hayes**
BLOOD OF A BOSS **I, II, III, IV, V**
SHADOWS OF THE GAME
By **Askari**
THE STREETS BLEED MURDER **I, II & III**
THE HEART OF A GANGSTA I II& III
By **Jerry Jackson**
CUM FOR ME I II III IV V VI
An **LDP Erotica Collaboration**
BRIDE OF A HUSTLA **I II & II**
THE FETTI GIRLS **I, II& III**
CORRUPTED BY A GANGSTA I, II III, IV
BLINDED BY HIS LOVE
THE PRICE YOU PAY FOR LOVE
DOPE GIRL MAGIC I II III
By **Destiny Skai**
WHEN A GOOD GIRL GOES BAD
By **Adrienne**
THE COST OF LOYALTY I II III
By Kweli

188

A GANGSTER'S REVENGE **I II III & IV**

THE BOSS MAN'S DAUGHTERS I II III IV V

A SAVAGE LOVE **I & II**

BAE BELONGS TO ME I II

A HUSTLER'S DECEIT I, II, III

WHAT BAD BITCHES DO I, II, III

SOUL OF A MONSTER I II III

KILL ZONE

A DOPE BOY'S QUEEN I II

By **Aryanna**

A KINGPIN'S AMBITON

A KINGPIN'S AMBITION **II**

I MURDER FOR THE DOUGH

By **Ambitious**

TRUE SAVAGE I II III IV V VI VII

DOPE BOY MAGIC I, II, III

MIDNIGHT CARTEL I II III

CITY OF KINGZ

By **Chris Green**

A DOPEBOY'S PRAYER

By **Eddie "Wolf" Lee**

THE KING CARTEL **I, II & III**

By **Frank Gresham**

THESE NIGGAS AIN'T LOYAL **I, II & III**

By **Nikki Tee**

GANGSTA SHYT **I II &III**

By **CATO**

Chris Green

THE ULTIMATE BETRAYAL
By **Phoenix**
BOSS'N UP **I , II & III**
By **Royal Nicole**
I LOVE YOU TO DEATH
By Destiny J
I RIDE FOR MY HITTA
I STILL RIDE FOR MY HITTA
By **Misty Holt**
LOVE & CHASIN' PAPER
By **Qay Crockett**
TO DIE IN VAIN
SINS OF A HUSTLA
By **ASAD**
BROOKLYN HUSTLAZ
By **Boogsy Morina**
BROOKLYN ON LOCK I & II
By **Sonovia**
GANGSTA CITY
By **Teddy Duke**
A DRUG KING AND HIS DIAMOND I & II III
A DOPEMAN'S RICHES
HER MAN, MINE'S TOO I, II
CASH MONEY HO'S
THE WIFEY I USED TO BE
By Nicole Goosby
TRAPHOUSE KING **I II & III**

KINGPIN KILLAZ I II III
STREET KINGS I II
PAID IN BLOOD **I II**
CARTEL KILLAZ I II III
DOPE GODS I II
By **Hood Rich**
LIPSTICK KILLAH **I, II, III**
CRIME OF PASSION I II & III
FRIEND OR FOE I II
By **Mimi**
STEADY MOBBN' **I, II, III**
THE STREETS STAINED MY SOUL
By **Marcellus Allen**
WHO SHOT YA **I, II, III**
SON OF A DOPE FIEND I II
Renta
GORILLAZ IN THE BAY **I II III IV**
TEARS OF A GANGSTA I II
3X KRAZY I II
DE'KARI
TRIGGADALE I II III
Elijah R. Freeman
GOD BLESS THE TRAPPERS I, II, III
THESE SCANDALOUS STREETS I, II, III
FEAR MY GANGSTA I, II, III IV, V
THESE STREETS DON'T LOVE NOBODY I, II
BURY ME A G I, II, III, IV, V

A GANGSTA'S EMPIRE I, II, III, IV

THE DOPEMAN'S BODYGAURD I II

THE REALEST KILLAZ I II III

Tranay Adams

THE STREETS ARE CALLING

Duquie Wilson

MARRIED TO A BOSS… I II III

By Destiny Skai & Chris Green

KINGZ OF THE GAME I II III IV V

Playa Ray

SLAUGHTER GANG I II III

RUTHLESS HEART I II III

By Willie Slaughter

FUK SHYT

By Blakk Diamond

DON'T F#CK WITH MY HEART I II

By Linnea

ADDICTED TO THE DRAMA I II III

IN THE ARM OF HIS BOSS II

By Jamila

YAYO I II III IV

A SHOOTER'S AMBITION I II

By S. Allen

TRAP GOD I II III

By Troublesome

FOREVER GANGSTA

GLOCKS ON SATIN SHEETS I II

By Adrian Dulan

TOE TAGZ I II III

LEVELS TO THIS SHYT

By Ah'Million

KINGPIN DREAMS I II

By Paper Boi Rari

CONFESSIONS OF A GANGSTA I II III

By Nicholas Lock

I'M NOTHING WITHOUT HIS LOVE

SINS OF A THUG

By Monet Dragun

CAUGHT UP IN THE LIFE I II III

By Robert Baptiste

NEW TO MONEY, MURDER & MEMORIES

THE GAME I II III

By **Malik D. Rice**

LIFE OF A SAVAGE I II III

A GANGSTA'S QUR'AN I II III

MURDA SEASON I II III

GANGLAND CARTEL I II

CHI'RAQ GANGSTAS I II

By **Romell Tukes**

LOYALTY AIN'T PROMISED I II

By Keith Williams

QUIET MONEY I II III

THUG LIFE I II

EXTENDED CLIP

Chris Green

By **Trai'Quan**

THE STREETS MADE ME I II

By **Larry D. Wright**

THE ULTIMATE SACRIFICE I, II, III, IV, V, VI

KHADIFI

IF YOU CROSS ME ONCE

ANGEL I II

By **Anthony Fields**

THE LIFE OF A HOOD STAR

By **Ca$h & Rashia Wilson**

THE STREETS WILL NEVER CLOSE

By **K'ajji**

CREAM

By **Yolanda Moore**

NIGHTMARES OF A HUSTLA I II

By **King Dream**

CONCRETE KILLAZ

By **Kingpen**

HARD AND RUTHLESS

By **Von Wiley Hall**

GHOST MOB II

Stilloan Robinson

MOB TIES

By **SayNoMore**

BOOKS BY LDP'S CEO, CA$H

TRUST IN NO MAN

TRUST IN NO MAN 2

TRUST IN NO MAN 3

BONDED BY BLOOD

SHORTY GOT A THUG

THUGS CRY

THUGS CRY 2

THUGS CRY 3

TRUST NO BITCH

TRUST NO BITCH 2

TRUST NO BITCH 3

TIL MY CASKET DROPS

RESTRAINING ORDER

RESTRAINING ORDER 2

IN LOVE WITH A CONVICT

LIFE OF A HOOD STAR

Chris Green

www.ingramcontent.com/pod-product-compliance
Lightning Source LLC
Chambersburg PA
CBHW070511260626
47161CB00004B/1521